"Easy...
take it easy, Zen."

Damon's warm breath tickled her neck as a strong arm clasped around her middle.

"I don't need help." She tugged at his fingers, finally freeing herself.

"What's wrong with you now?" He rubbed the back of his hand, his eyes narrowing on her. "You're like an emotional chameleon. I never know what mood you'll be in next."

"Then ignore me." She whirled away from him, her emotions in chaos. But an iron hand reached out, and Damon pulled her back against him.

"Damn you, Zen," he muttered. He found her mouth, and his tongue penetrated to tease hers before he took full possession. His other hand slid to the small of her back and pressed her intimately against him. "Damn you, Zen," he repeated.

Dear Reader:

Three months ago we were delighted to announce the arrival of TO HAVE AND TO HOLD, the thrilling new romance series that takes you into the world of married love. We're pleased to report that letters of praise and enthusiasm are pouring in daily. TO HAVE AND TO HOLD is clearly off to a great start!

TO HAVE AND TO HOLD is the first and only series that portrays the joys and heartaches of marriage. Its unique concept makes it significantly different from the other lines now available to you, and it presents stories that meet the high standards set by SECOND CHANCE AT LOVE. TO HAVE AND TO HOLD offers all the compelling romance, exciting sensuality, and heartwarming entertainment you expect.

We think you'll love TO HAVE AND TO HOLD—and that you'll become the kind of loyal reader who is making SECOND CHANCE AT LOVE an ever-increasing success. Read about love affairs that last a lifetime. Look for three TO HAVE AND TO HOLD romances each and every month, as well as six SECOND CHANCE AT LOVE romances each month. We hope you'll read and enjoy them all. And please keep writing! Your thoughts about our books are very important to us.

Warm wishes,

Ellen Edwards

Ellen Edwards
SECOND CHANCE AT LOVE
The Berkley Publishing Group
200 Madison Avenue
New York, N.Y. 10016

Second Chance at Love.

NO GENTLE POSSESSION

ANN CRISTY

SECOND CHANCE AT LOVE
BOOK

Other books by *Ann Cristy*

Second Chance at Love
FROM THE TORRID PAST   #49
TORN ASUNDER   #60
ENTHRALLED   #103

To Have and to Hold
TREAD SOFTLY   #3

Damn the man; he is my albatross...

Chapter 1

"ARE YOU TIRED, Aunt Zeno?" Seven-year-old David clasped Zen Driscoll's arm as she leaned back in the cushioned seat and closed her eyes. The thought flashed through her mind that it was typical of the Aristides family to demand first-class air travel even for someone they didn't really want to see—herself.

"No, love, I'm not tired," she told David. "Just glad to be through the hassle of customs and on our way." Silently she added, I'm also nervous about leaving my job, which I love, to return for three months to a situation that I ran from three years ago.

She stared at David beside her. Large-boned, dark-haired, and dark-eyed, he had become her world. Seamus Dare, her friend and occasional escort, often told her she was too wrapped up in the boy, but even Seamus was not immune to David's charm.

"Will we ever come back to Dublin?" David asked, a faint quaver in his soft Irish brogue. Zen regarded him tenderly. Ireland had been his home for three years, ever

1

since she had taken him there at the age of four. As soon as she had been officially declared his guardian, she had leaped at the chance to take a job in Dublin with Deirdre Cable, the world-renowned designer of woolen fashions for women . . . and to leave the United States and Damon Aristides behind.

"Will Daniel remember me, Aunt Zeno?" David tugged on her arm and scooted to a kneeling position on the seat next to her.

"Yes, of course he will." Zen tried to sound more confident than she felt.

"Will Nonna Sophie remember me, too? And Uncle Damon?" David questioned with stubborn persistence.

"Of course they will. I've sent pictures of you to them, just as they sent pictures of Daniel to us."

"Oh." David nodded, but his brow was still creased. "Robbie says that if I have a twin, he's s'posed to live with me."

Zen felt a wrench in her chest. Robbie was right, she thought, pushing back a strand of David's black hair. "That's why we're going to America, so you can be with your twin brother Daniel." Zen tried to swallow the lump in her throat as David screwed up his face in thoughtful concentration. Finally his brow smoothed, and he nodded.

"Then we can bring Daniel back to Ireland with us, and he can play with Robbie, too," he concluded brightly.

David's words conjured up in Zen a vision of Damon Aristides as he'd looked that day three years ago, standing outside the courtroom just after she had won the right to take David to Ireland with her. Thrown into shadow, Damon's dark good looks had taken on a satanic cast.

"This isn't the end of it," he'd warned her angrily. "And don't think you'll ever have Daniel."

"Don't you dare threaten me! You're the one who forced this court fight, not I," Zen shot back. "As David's guardian, I was within my rights to petition to take him with me to Ireland."

Sophie, Damon's mother, came up to them and pleaded

for them to be calmer, more understanding. But Zen shook her head and walked away, knowing her emotions would spill over if she said one more word to anyone.

She and Damon had parted bitterly, leaving so many thoughts and feelings unsaid, refusing to acknowledge all that they had meant to each other.

Now, three years later, a much-changed Zen was flying back to Long Island and the Aristides estate in response to Damon's request that she come home. Sophie, he claimed, wanted to see David.

Zen wondered if Sophie would find her much changed. Through her association with the world of fashion Zen had acquired an aura of sophistication, a confidence and grace that made her feel like an entirely different woman from the Zen Driscoll Sophie had known. Zen knew she was good at what she did, and that she was getting better all the time, just as her name was becoming better known. Designing fabrics fulfilled an artistic need in her, just as caring for David fulfilled a need to love. She was content with her life in Dublin.

"We can bring Daniel to Ireland, can't we, Aunt Zeno?" David persisted, pulling on her sleeve and rousing her from her reverie.

"Ah, no, love, I doubt we can bring Daniel back to Ireland," she said.

"Just for a visit?" David thrust out his jaw and scowled at his aunt. "He'll want to see Dublin and Robbie and play football . . . I mean soccer."

Zen smiled at the boy. "We'll ask," she said, but her heart contracted painfully at the thought of making such a request of Damon. She pushed him out of her mind and concentrated on the boy at her side. She was proud of his healthy good looks and vibrant personality. David was already involved in a soccer club for boys. His close friend, Robbie Parnell, often visited their apartment in Dublin, which Zen rented from the design company she worked for.

"Did my daddy and mommy like you and Uncle Damon?" David asked, his eyes fixed on hers.

"Your mother, Eleni, was my older sister," Zen explained, "and your daddy, Davos, was Uncle Damon's younger brother."

"And that's why you take care of me and Uncle Damon and Nonna take care of Daniel," David recited proudly. "That's what I told Robbie, but he said twins should be together."

Zen saw that David's eyes were questioning her now, but would they accuse her someday? She tried to smother the guilt that assailed her. She was responsible for having separated the boys . . .

"Do you like Uncle Damon, Aunt Zeno?" David quizzed, playing with the buckle of his seat belt, then looking out the window.

Like him? Zen's brain reeled. *Like* could never describe the tumultuous, overwhelming relationship she had had with Damon Aristides. She tried to dispel the memory of a twenty-year-old Zen meeting him for the first time when they'd both been honor attendants at Eleni and Davos's wedding. In that one instant her life had changed forever.

"I admire Uncle Damon's business acumen," Zen stated truthfully.

"What's an ak-a-min?" David asked.

"It means your uncle is an intelligent man and a well-known shipping industrialist. He also owns an airline. His company is called Olympus Limited," Zen explained, half wishing David would stop asking questions.

"Is this his airplane, Aunt Zeno?" David was looking out the window, watching the swirl of fluffy clouds that formed a blanket beneath the plane.

"Not this plane, but others like it." Zen masked a sigh. She was tired of speaking of the great Damon Aristides, an American born of Greek parents, a man who, in her opinion, still held an archaic view of women.

She tried not to think of him, but her mind betrayed her and carried her back to that day at Eleni and Davos's wedding when Damon had taken her arm as they followed the bride and groom back up the aisle. The way she remembered it, he had not released her hand for the rest of the day.

The next day she had returned to college in upstate New York, sure she would never see him again. But she hadn't been able to get him out of her mind.

At her sister's insistence Zen had stayed with Eleni and Davos on her holiday break. Since the young women had no other relatives, they were very close.

Each time Zen stayed at Eleni's, Damon arrived and took her to a show or dancing. But, although Zen wanted desperately for him to be more than courteous, more than friendly, he never kissed her, hardly ever touched her. Then, one day soon after she turned twenty-one, and just before she graduated, she went sailing with Damon. They dropped anchor and swam off the side of the boat, then went down to the cabin to change.

Their relationship had always been stormy, full of emotional highs and lows, but this time something seemed to snap in Damon. Like a dam bursting, he lost control and swept her into his arms, both cursing and muttering endearments to her. The moments had run together in a pleasure-filled blur as he initiated her into the tender joys of physical love. His touch had left her breathless and totally committed to him. He became the center of her existence.

Zen moved restlessly in her seat as she remembered. Oh, the arguments they had had! How often she had run away from him ... then back to mend the rift. How wild and passionate their reunions had been.

How he had comforted her that day when the twins were three-and-a-half years old—the day Davos and Eleni had died in a sailing accident. She and Damon had stood close together when the will was read, and they'd learned that they were to share custody of the boys. She was named David's guardian; Damon was named Daniel's guardian. If they married, they would become the boys' legal parents.

They had supported each other in their grief until the day Damon's Aunt Dalia had informed Zen that Damon had another woman in New York, a woman he kept in an apartment. Zen would have laughed in her face if Damon's mother, who had been standing nearby and overheard, had not flushed a deep red.

"Is it true, Mrs. Aristides?" Zen had begged. "You were my mother's friend. As her daughter, I ask you to tell me the truth."

Sophie had remained silent.

"Why should she tell you anything?" Dalia had interjected. "As for your mother, young lady, she married beneath her... an artist from Greenwich Village, a man who was not even Greek."

A shaken Zen had lashed out at her. "My father was a successful painter. My parents were happy. They made our lives wonderful..." Zen swallowed painfully. "When the plane crashed they were on their way to Paris for a showing of my father's works. The money from the sales paid for Eleni's and my education."

She could see in her mind's eye a younger Zen storming out of the room, confronting Damon that very night with the charges his aunt had made. "And do you keep a woman?" she shouted.

"You're often angry with me, Xenobia," he said. "Should I be without a woman's company at those times?" Damon regarded her haughtily. "When we are not together, it's none of your business what I do." His body was taut with anger.

"Damn you, Damon Aristides!" Zen whirled away from him. She didn't answer his phone calls, and she refused to see him when he came to her apartment. When Deirdre Cable offered her a job, she sought a court order to retain custody of David and left for Ireland.

"What is Seamus doing now, Aunt Zeno?" David asked, interrupting her painful thoughts. He yawned and blinked, the long trip beginning to take its toll.

Zen glanced at her watch. "I suppose he'll be sitting down to his dinner soon."

"I like Uncle Seamus. He knows how to play football... I mean soccer... and he said he would like a boy like me," David pronounced proudly.

"So he did, and I don't blame him." Zen hugged her nephew, who hugged her back. Zen welcomed the obvious affection he had for her.

"Would Seamus like Daniel?" David waited expectantly for her answer.

"I'm sure he would," she assured him.

"Then if you marry Seamus, Daniel can come live with us, can't he?" The idea had taken firm root in his mind.

"Honey, Seamus and I have not been talking about getting married." Zen noted the stubborn thrust of David's chin, which was so like his father's . . . and his uncle's.

"But if you did, he could, couldn't he?" David persisted, worrying the question like a dog with a bone.

"Yes, of course he could."

"Good. I'd like having my own playmate living with me."

"I know you would." Zen kissed David's cheek, loving him, pleased with the grin he gave her.

The trip was long and tiring and, despite the many distractions offered by the flight attendants, David grew restless and cranky. By the time they had landed and gone through customs, he was complaining frequently and loudly.

"I don't like it here." He pushed out his lower lip and scowled at his aunt as they reached the baggage claim area.

"We'll be there soon. You'll feel better after a nap," Zen said absently, searching for their luggage on the moving conveyor belt.

David stopped in his tracks and twisted out of her grip.

"I don't want to take a nap. I want to go home and play with Robbie."

"Listen here, young man . . ." Zen bent to grab his arm, but he moved swiftly out of her reach just as she spotted her suitcase. "David, come back here or—"

"Can't you control him better than that?" a deep,

masculine voice interrupted, sending a frisson of panic up Zen's spine just as she swung her overnight case off the conveyor belt. She caught Damon Aristides in the midsection with a resounding thwack. He doubled up, all the breath knocked out of him.

Zen stared in dismay, then all her long-repressed anger at Damon Aristides boiled to the surface. "Well, it serves you right for startling me that way," she said stiffly, thrusting out her jaw. "Anyway, it was an accident."

Damon straightened, grimacing with pain and irritation. "It always is . . . an accident, I mean. You are the most dangerous person to be around."

Zen inhaled sharply at the full sight of him and swooped to retrieve David's suitcase as it moved past her. "I only have accidents with you," she retorted somewhat breathlessly. "David, please mind your suitcase while I get the others."

"For God's sake, let me take those," Damon interrupted. "Yanos, get the other cases," he told the liveried chauffeur at his shoulder.

"Is he Uncle Damon?" David asked in an awed stage whisper. "Is he the one you don't like?"

Zen flushed with embarrassment. She had never discussed her personal feelings for the members of the Aristides family. It occurred to her that children were far more perceptive than adults gave them credit for being. She stared in wonder up at Damon as his face grew taut with anger and his eyes glinted darkly.

He seemed bigger, more threatening than she remembered, all black like the Brian Boru of Irish folklore— hair, eyes, brows, even the curling hair that could be seen at the cuffs of his shirt. He was tall and broad-chested with high cheekbones and steely muscles. His body was conditioned to fighting form, Zen thought, her heart plummeting. She struggled to keep her courage high. She damn well wouldn't let him intimidate her.

Her heart squeezed into a knot when she saw the gray hair at his temples, but the rest of it was still black and thick and straight as it had always been. His huge body dwarfed her tiny frame, and his dark coloring contrasted sharply with her curly blond-red hair, brown eyes, and white skin.

God, he looked angry! She'd better try to explain. "David meant—"

"I'm sure I know what he meant." Damon's harsh words stunned her into silence. "Shall we go? Yanos will bring the luggage to the car."

"He might not find my soccer ball." David stood with his legs apart, looking belligerently up at the man who had yet to speak to him.

Damon studied him for a long moment, then squatted down in front of him, showing a careless unconcern for his pearl gray cashmere suit, which molded itself to his body as though it had been sewn on him. "You're a soccer player, are you?" he said softly. "I used to play soccer."

"You did?" David's expression lightened.

"Yes. Perhaps between the two of us we can convince your brother to play, too." He paused, touching the boy's cheek with one finger. "You look like Daniel, but I think you may be just a little bigger. You're older, you know. By three minutes."

"I know. Aunt Zeno told me." David pushed out his chest. "I'm as big as Robbie . . . almost . . . and he's the biggest boy on our team."

"That's great." Damon rose to his feet, holding David's hand in his. "Don't worry about your ball. Yanos is very thorough."

They headed for the exit, but David stopped and looked anxiously back at Zen. "You come too, Aunt Zeno." There was a quaver in his voice.

"I'm right behind you, love." Zen deliberately avoided Damon's intense gaze.

"That's good." The boy looked up at Damon. He did not free his hand, but a stubborn expression came over his face again. "I live with my Aunt Zeno. She takes care of me."

"I see," Damon said, looking from the boy to Zen,

who stood several feet away. "Come along . . . Aunt Zeno."

David looked relieved. Avoiding Damon's eyes, Zen stepped to the other side of David and took his other hand.

In the limousine, David chattered with excitement, asking endless questions and supplying random bits of information about himself. He exclaimed repeatedly over the vehicle's special features and kept Yanos busy explaining how they worked. Zen was soon lost in her own thoughts. Just seeing Damon had stirred memories she'd thought long dead . . .

"How are you?" Damon's terse question startled her. She stared blankly at him. "There's no need to be frightened," he snarled, his voice low.

"I'm not frightened of you or your family," Zen snapped, alert now. "I was just thinking of someone . . . something." Her voice trailed off. She wasn't sure what she had been thinking.

"Ah, yes, the boyfriend . . ." His soft voice was underlaid with steel.

"Why don't we agree not to talk about personal matters?" she suggested frostily, struggling to keep her anger from her voice.

"How can we not discuss personal matters when you have custody of *my* nephew," he retorted.

"And you have custody of *my* nephew," Zen riposted.

"True. And since I will be marrying in the near future, my mother feels I could provide a better home for—"

"Not on your life!" Fury curled through Zen like smoke from a forest fire. "If that's what it takes, then I'll marry Seamus." She said his name without thinking. "Then I'll be able to provide a home for Daniel as well as for David."

"Seamus? He's the man you're involved with?" Damon's words dropped like bombs.

"Seamus and I are not *involved,* as you put it, but David likes him, and so do I."

"Don't you dare subject David to your series of lovers." Damon said the words as if he were throwing spears.

"Then I'll marry Seamus," Zen said with measured sweetness, wishing Damon would leave her alone.

David turned to face her, a pleased smile on his face. "You *are* going to marry Seamus? Goodo! Then I can live in Dublin again, and Daniel can come live with us . . . maybe. I like Seamus," he added wistfully before leaning forward again to ask Yanos how fast the car could go.

Zen didn't look at Damon, but the goose bumps on her skin warned her of his anger. "You shouldn't listen to David."

"Don't tell me what I should or shouldn't do," Damon said stiffly.

Zen glared at him, then shifted away and stared sightlessly out the window.

David didn't seem bothered by their strained silence. He continued to hit Yanos with a barrage of questions. The old man answered him patiently. "This car doesn't have the best mileage, but—"

"Why does it need twelve cylinders?" David asked.

By the time they reached the Aristides estate, a huge gray stone building on Long Island's north shore, Zen was ready to jump out of her skin with impatience.

With effort she stilled a fluttering panic when she saw Sophie Aristides standing on the fan-shaped cement steps leading to the front entranceway, a slightly smaller version of David standing next to her. Sophie's hand lay possessively on Daniel's shoulder.

As the car drew up, Zen pulled David down next to her on the seat. "There's your grandmother and your brother Daniel," she whispered, her hands tightening on his shoulders.

"Oh," David whsipered back, all at once quiet as they got out of the car and stood uncertainly in the driveway.

For a moment Zen felt a fiery resentment because Sophie stood three steps above them, like a queen looking down on her subjects. Zen bit her lip, deliberately pushing aside those feelings. Suddenly, looking up at Daniel, she felt a great rush of love for the boy.

"Hello, I'm your Aunt Xenobia. But you can call me Aunt Zeno, as David does." Zen paused, studying the boy. He looked very much like David, but there was a subtle difference. David had the stockier build of the Aristides, while Daniel was smaller with somewhat lighter skin and a more delicate facial structure, like his mother Eleni. Yes, Zen thought, there was more Driscoll in Daniel than in his twin.

"Hello." Daniel's smile was like sun coming through clouds on a rainy day.

David responded instantly. "Hi." He bounded up three steps. "Do you like football?" he asked, referring to the soccer of Ireland, the Irish lilt in his voice sounding more pronounced.

"Oh, I do," Daniel replied quietly. "I've been to see the New York Jets."

"Huh? Do they play for the World Cup, Aunt Zeno?" David asked, clearly puzzled.

"No, darling. Remember I told you that in this country football is called soccer."

"I forgot," he said solemnly, but with a twinkle in his eye as he came back down the steps and took her hand.

Zen turned him around. "Now go back and say hello to your grandmother."

"Oh . . . that's right." David ran and grabbed Sophie's right hand. "How do you do, Grandmother, I hope you're well," he recited, just as Zen had taught him. He laughed up at the stern-faced, older woman, totally at ease with her. "Are you going to kiss me now?"

Sophie's rigid expression softened; then she seemed to collect herself. She leaned down and kissed David's cheek. "You are full of vinegar, I can see that. Do you speak Greek? Your brother Daniel does."

"Mother," Damon said softly but firmly, "it's not necessary for the boy to know Greek since both of them will be speaking English."

"That's all right. I don't mind teaching David to speak Greek," Daniel offered with a maturity beyond his years.

"Okay," David said with a shrug, "but not now." Zen

followed his gaze across the wide expanse of manicured lawn that sloped gently down to Long Island Sound. "We can play foot—I mean soccer—here. There's lots' of room."

"After you change your clothes...After you visit with your grandmother...After your rest," Zen told him.

"Aunt Zeno," David wailed. "All those things to do first...I'll never get to play." He pushed out his chin, and glared at Zen, but she remained firm. "All right," he relented, "but I won't like it." He hung his head and paced the stone step, scowling, then grimaced at his twin. "Aunt Zeno is nice, but when she makes up her mind, ya havta go along." David's brogue thickened emotionally as he and Daniel stepped into the cavernous house, following a butler.

Zen studied Sophie's steel-colored hair and black shoe-button eyes and thought she looked much the same as she had three years ago. She had a few more lines in her majestic face, but she stood as straight and as strong as ever.

"Hello, Mrs. Aristides," Zen said. "It's been a long time." Zen was surprised at how stiff her words sounded. She was finding it hard to face this woman.

"Hello, Xenobia. You look well...and prosperous. You didn't used to style your long hair like that...or wear such high heels. You've grown up."

"I'm twenty-eight years old," Zen replied defensively.

Sophie regarded her in thoughtful silence. "The April wind has a chill," she finally said. "Why don't we go inside?" She turned regally and walked slowly into the house.

Following, Zen was temporarily blinded by the suddenly dim light after the bright sunshine. She stumbled slightly and instantly felt a hand at her waist. Stiffening, she pulled away and glanced up.

Damon's face was hard as granite. "You didn't always pull away from me," he said softly but with underlying steel.

"That was in another lifetime." Zen backe
and turned to face him. "I'm not some moor

you can manipulate like a puppet on a string." His angry expression made her take another involuntary step backward.

"You—" He stopped, then gestured to a servant to help Yanos take the baggage upstairs.

Released from the gaze of Damon's impenetrable black eyes, Zen hastened toward the sound of the boys' voices in the living room.

Tea had been served, but, ignoring it, the boys stood facing each other on a Persian carpet. David was tossing a hard roll from hand to hand, and his grandmother was sitting straight-backed on a settee in front of the tea trolley, watching him.

Mouth agape, Zen stared immobilized as David threw the roll into the air and butted it with his head like a soccer ball.

"Now you try it," he instructed his twin.

Daniel sailed his hard roll into the air and dived toward it, head first. He missed it by a wide margin and reeled into a Sheraton table, knocking over an Ainsley lamp.

Zen leaped forward, reaching out to save the lamp just as Damon stepped in front of her. Her hand grazed his cheek moments before he deftly righted the lamp.

"Zen!" he thundered, his right hand coming up to cover the scratched cheek at the same time that her forward momentum thrust her against his rock-hard chest. They staggered, his body absorbing the full impact of hers, then stumbled into a chair. Zen landed sprawled in Damon's lap. His arms tightened immediately around her as they gasped for breath.

"Crikey, Aunt Zeno, look what you did to Uncle Damon's face." David's loud voice echoed in the suddenly quiet room. "She doesn't do things like this at home," he informed his open-mouthed twin. Then he smiled at his grandmother. "Sometimes Aunt Zeno plays soccer with me, though."

"I see." Sophie Aristides had risen to her feet and was regarding with disapproval the tangle of legs and arms on her high-backed silk chair. "Damon, do get up. Xenobia, you will cover your legs." The boys giggled, and Damon muttered darkly.

"Mother," he began, trying to set Zen on her feet, "I think you should pour the boys something to drink." His face was flushed with anger when he stood at last and met his mother's enigmatic expression.

"I do not believe that tea or chocolate would have enticed the boys away from the intriguing sight of their aunt and uncle behaving like children in the living room." Ignoring her son's flaring nostrils and clenched teeth, Sophie put a hand on the shoulder of each boy and urged them toward the tea trolley. "There are homemade biscuits and cookies." She hesitated when she saw David mask a yawn with his hand. "After tea, I will rest before dinner. You may come up and talk with me, David. Daniel might like to speak to Aunt Zeno."

Daniel smiled hesitantly at Zen, melting her anger and making her heart twist with love. In that instant, he looked so like Eleni.

Zen took a chair across from Sophie and close to David, who sat cross-legged on a cushion and began eating a biscuit covered with strawberry jam.

When Damon sat down, both boys stared at the scratch on his cheek. Sophie regarded it also, but said nothing. Embarrassed by what she'd done, but feeling angry and resentful toward Damon, who she didn't trust for one moment, Zen studied the pattern in her damask napkin.

A few minutes later a plump woman in her fifties with black hair streaked with gray entered the room. She bestowed a warm smile on the boys and told them to come with her. Zen recognized the housekeeper who had been with the Aristides family for as long as she had known them.

David hesitated and glanced at Zen.

"You needn't mind, young mister," the woman said. "I'm Lona, and I'm going to show you which room is yours, and then you may go along to your grandmother's room, or wherever you like."

"All right, but I want to sleep near Aunt Zeno. Sometimes she gets nightmares...and I take care of her," David said.

Zen's stomach seemed to drop to her toes. She knew David was trying to hide his own nervousness, but she dreaded Damon's reaction to his revelation.

Lona inclined her head and assured him he would be close to his Aunt Zeno. The boys left side by side, Lona leading the way.

Silence fell over the room like a shroud.

Sophie cleared her throat, the sound loud in the abrupt stillness. "So...you have nightmares, Xenobia?"

Zen coughed nervously. "I did...a few times." She had no wish to discuss the bad dreams that had caused her many restless nights.

"No doubt from losing your sister so tragically," Sophie mused.

Zen nodded, determined never to tell anyone what had caused her nightmares...never to describe the long struggle to overcome them.

"More coffee, Damon?" Sophie's voice was calm, unruffled.

Damon held out his cup, his expression unreadable.

"Tell me about your work, Xenobia." Mrs. Aristides poured more tea for Zen.

"I'm an assistant designer with Deirdre Cable, of Cable Knits Limited, Dublin. Occasionally I design suits or dresses, but mostly I design fabric. I work closely with the weavers. I love my job, and I make a good living for David and myself." She took a deep breath. "I'm on leave for three months."

"You haven't married."

"No."

"Damon is getting married, next year perhaps, to a Melissa Harewell."

"That name doesn't sound Greek," Zen snapped, then bit her lip.

Damon glared at her. "Lissa's bloodlines do not concern me, or should they you," he said. "Her family has been in this country since the Pilgrims."

"Ah ... you mean she's descended from the thieves and reprobates who first settled this country."

Damon rounded on her. "You're twisting my words, Zen."

"It's strange that I didn't see her picture in the *New York Times*," Zen went on, seemingly unperturbed. "I get it in Dublin." She took a sip of tea.

"We haven't formally announced it yet." Damon grimaced at his mother, who placidly dropped two lumps of sugar into his coffee. "Mother, I never take sugar."

"Perhaps she thinks you need to add something sweet to your system," Zen shot at him.

"You haven't changed, Zen," he accused her. "Still the same sharp tongue you've always had." He took a sip of coffee and choked. "Mother, I'd like another cup."

"Of course."

Zen set down her tea. "I think I'll go up and see how David is."

"No need," Sophie said swiftly. "Do tell me about the man you intend to marry."

"Mother, Zen never said she was marrying," Damon said coldly.

"I think it would be good for her to marry. It's difficult to raise a boy alone. Of course once *you* are married, you will be in a position to take both boys."

"Never!" Zen surged to her feet. "If you think I would let you take David from me—"

"I've never said anything like—" Damon protested.

"Then why did your mother—"

Damon jumped to his feet as well. "My mother and I have never discussed taking David from you."

"You can't. Don't forget that. That was all thrashed out in court three years ago when I obtained permission to take him to Ireland." Zen faced him, arms akimbo, her eyes snapping fire at him.

"Why do you keep reading things into what I say?" Damon demanded.

"Because I know you, and I'm going to be watching you all the time. Seamus—"

"Don't bring his name into it!"

"Stop shouting! You sound like a dockworker." Zen shook her fist in his face as his mother's hand hovered delicately over the cookie tray.

"And you sound like an Irish washerwoman."

"Don't you make fun of the Irish," Zen shouted, furious.

"I wasn't making fun of the Irish; I was drawing an analogy," Damon explained in a low roar as his mother dabbed calmly at her lips with a napkin.

"Bushwaugh!" Zen riposted.

Sophie looked up with mild curiosity. "Is that an Irish curseword?" she asked.

"No!" Damon and Zen shouted together, looking at her, then back at each other.

"Oh," said Sophie.

Damon took a deep breath, drawing Zen's eyes to his breadth of shoulder. "We invited you here so that the boys would have a chance to get acquainted. Isn't that right, Mother?"

"Hmm? Oh, yes. I think it would be a fine idea for Xenobia to see how well the two boys would fit into the life you and Melissa are planning." She finished on a sigh, putting a tiny, cherry-filled crepe into her mouth and closing her eyes in enjoyment.

"Mother!" Damon stared at her.

"I am not letting you have David! I would not have come here if I'd known I would be subjected to this kind of aggravation." Zen took a deep breath to continue, but Damon interrupted.

"Aggravation!" he stormed. "What do you call what you did to me at the airport today?"

"Oh? What was that?" Sophie asked, stirring her Turkish coffee in small, precise circles.

"She struck me . . . in the stomach," Damon muttered, not taking his eyes from Zen.

"Really?" Sophie's narrow mouth twitched once, as though she were stifling a smile.

"It was a little lower than that, I think. In the groin, perhaps?" Zen clarified with great relish, glancing at his mother. "Anyway, it was an accident." She looked back at Damon. "I told you that." She lifted her chin defiantly.

"Accident? Bull! I see now that you deliberately tried to incapacitate me."

"Only in the bedroom," Zen riposted, then felt her face flush with embarrassment as she remembered his mother's presence.

But Sophie was busy studying the cookie tray and seemed not to have heard.

"It will be a cold day in hell when you can put me out of commission in bed," Damon said. His eyes had a coal-hard sheen that seemed to pierce to her inner core and spark an inexplicable emotion.

"Who cares what you do in . . . anywhere!" Zen cried.

They stood staring at each other, the strength of their antipathy . . . and some other feeling . . . making them oblivious to everything but each other.

"You are a guest in my house, and as such you will be treated with respect and courtesy."

"Just as you would treat the family goat on the island of Keros?" Zen shot back.

"Stop acting as though we were born in Greece. You were born here, just as I was." Damon struggled visibly to control his temper.

"I was born in Selkirk, New York, not on Long Island," Zen pointed out childishly.

"Oh, I don't think you've changed much," Sophie said into the sudden silence. "Xenobia still has that turned-up nose, which is so un-Greek."

"Many people prefer a turned-up nose," Damon said.

"Not Greeks." His mother shrugged.

"You do not speak for all Greeks," her son thundered. "Besides, this is the United States."

"I am pleased, my son, that your geography lessons were not wasted on you."

Damon's teeth snapped together as he studied his mother, baffled anger twisting his classic features.

"And, of course, Xenobia's endearing habit of attacking you at every turn—"

"She doesn't do that."

"I don't do that."

Damon and Zen spoke at the same time.

Sophie shrugged. "Well, how would you describe that little scene when she scratched your cheek, then fell into your lap with her skirt riding up to her thighs? I cannot say I approve." She selected another sweet.

"It was an accident," Damon growled.

Suddenly Zen had had enough. "Excuse me. I think I'll go to my room," she said through clenched teeth. "I assume it's the same one I had before." She stalked out of the living room before either Damon or Sophie could answer.

Chapter 2

IT WOULD HAVE been an exaggeration to say that the Aristides' home was in a state of siege, but in the days that followed Zen found the atmosphere distinctly unfriendly—except where the two boys were concerned.

Not only had they become friends but David, who had never been interested in anything but games, was trying hard to learn Greek; and Daniel, who, as he told Zen, had never cared for sports, was discovering he had a natural ability at soccer.

The next afternoon, Zen was playing goalie as the boys brought the soccer ball down the field toward the net that Yanos had constructed for them. The ground was damp from a morning drizzle, and the grass was slippery. As the ball sped toward Zen, she dived to repel it, but suddenly she lost her footing and crashed against the uprights holding the net.

She stood up slowly, feeling a little shaken and cradling her left arm, where she knew a bruise would show the next day. Suddenly she was swung up into powerful arms.

Her senses reeled. Her head bounced against a hard shoulder as her rescuer began running for the house. "Damon! Damon, stop it. Put me down. I'm not hurt."

He slowed to a stop, the boys puffing up behind him, but he didn't release her. His eyes swept intently over her, seeming to check every pore.

"Is Aunt Zeno hurt, Uncle Damon?" Daniel asked anxiously.

"Naw," David answered. "Aunt Zeno doesn't get hurt, do you?" David looked up at his aunt as she lay cradled in Damon's arms.

"No, of course I don't. Damon, you can put me down now." She pushed against his steellike body.

"Do you like being carried, Aunt Zeno?" David frowned up at her. "When I grow up, I can carry you, too."

"I wouldn't want you to, dear." She smiled down at the boy, then looked up at Damon. "Will you put me down?" she insisted. She glanced toward the house and groaned as Sophie stepped onto the terrace, watching them.

"Nonna," Daniel called, "Aunt Zeno fell."

"She's always falling...or something," Sophie agreed calmly.

"Ohh!" Zen pushed against Damon with all her strength. "I can walk, you big oaf," she snapped. His eyes riveted on hers, he let her legs drop to the ground, but he continued to hold her close with one arm.

"You were shaken in the fall. I saw it," Damon insisted, staring tenderly down at her. "I was coming up the drive in my car."

Sophie who was strolling toward them, heard his comment. "And you drove your car over my best rambling roses, too." She pointed disdainfully toward the Ferrari, which was parked in the middle of the rose bed. "Usually she manages to get you, Damon, my son, but this time she got my roses." Sophie glanced placidly at the boys, who were watching the adults. "You must be hungry, boys. Come inside. Lona has cool drinks for you." She shepherded them in front of her, not looking back.

"Your mother has a way of twisting reality to suit her own purposes," Zen observed.

Damon shrugged. "She may not be tactful, but she is kind."

"Kind of what? Kind of nasty? Kind of spiteful? She never stops making remarks about...about my..."

"Clumsiness?" Damon suggested.

Zen lifted her chin defiantly. "Now, listen here, Damon Aristides. I'll have you know that I never had the least trouble when I was living in Ireland."

"I wonder why that is," he mused, his eyes making an intent study of her hair. "Do you know your hair is fiery in the sunlight?"

"I never had the least problem hitting people, falling on...My hair?" She lifted a hand to her head, feeling how the waves had tightened into ringlets. "I'm a mess. I'd better take a shower." The quaver in her voice annoyed her.

"You should," Damon agreed, taking her arm and holding it close to him. "I'll go with you. I want to shower and change, too."

As they entered the door at the back of the house Damon curved his arm around her waist and kept it there as he led her through the kitchen, where he spoke to Lona and a heavy woman he called Maria. "Here." He opened a door, showing Zen a back stairway.

She could feel him behind her as they climbed the stairs, almost as though his arm were still around her. All at once, with blinding clarity, she remembered herself as the young woman who had sought the touch of Damon Aristides, who wasn't happy unless his strong hands were caressing and arousing her to fierce intensity. Sucking in her breath, she began taking the stairs two at a time.

"Easy...take it easy, Zen." His warm breath tickled her neck as a strong arm clasped around her middle.

"I don't need help." She tugged at his fingers, finally freeing herself as they reached the upstairs hall that led to the wing where the boys' rooms and hers were located.

Damon's apartment was reached through double doors
that led to his private corridor. His was the largest section
of the house and totally separate from the sleeping quarters of the rest of the family and guests.

"What's wrong with you now?" He rubbed the back
of his hand, his eyes narrowing on her. "You're like an
emotional chameleon. I never know what mood you'll
be in next."

"Then ignore me." She whirled away from him, her
emotions in chaos. But an iron hand reached out, and
Damon pulled her back against him, his two hands coming up and around to cup her breasts, his mouth lowering
to her neck and nibbling there.

"Damn you, Zen," he muttered, his right hand leaving
her breast to raise her chin. He found her mouth, and
his tongue penetrated to tease hers and touch the inside
of her lips before he took full, demanding possession.
His other hand slid, palm flat, fingers spread, to the small
of her back and pressed her intimately against him. "Damn
you, Zen," he repeated.

He released her abruptly, and she staggered, disori-
ented. Then he was striding toward the double doors,
calling over his shoulder, "Melissa is coming to dinner
tonight. She wants to meet David." The doors slammed
behind him, the sound echoing down the oak-paneled
hall, freezing Zen in place.

"That...that...lecher!" She stood immobilized,
rubbing her mouth, not able to still the tremors that
wracked her body. "If he touches me again, I'll..."
Drawing in a shaky breath, she turned blindly toward
her room.

Her movements were stiff as she took off her clothes
and selected fresh underthings to bring into the bathroom.
As she stood under the shower spray, lathering her body
and shampooing her hair, she considered ingenious ways
of taking care of Damon Aristides.

She was sitting in front of her mirror putting on her
makeup when she decided to weight him with granite
and drop him in Long Island Sound.

"Why are you smiling, Aunt Zeno?" David asked from the doorway. She looked up to see Daniel at his side.

Zen turned on the vanity bench, her head still wrapped in a towel, and smiled at the two boys who were so alike yet so different. "I must have been thinking of you two if I was smiling. How did Lona manage to get you both dressed so fine?" Zen felt a twinge of annoyance at the worsted fabric of the boys' identical suits, but she pushed the emotion away. The pale blue tweed set off their bronzed skin and dark eyes. And if it gave Sophie pleasure to shop for them, Zen didn't have the heart to criticize her extravagance.

David looked down at himself, then grimaced at his aunt. "Lona promised Dan and me two of the éclairs that Maria's making for dessert tonight." Zen laughed, and David looked puzzled. Then he frowned. "Uncle Damon says we're not to play rough with you. Did we hurt you, Aunt Zeno?"

At the mention of Damon, Zen's body tensed. The man was diabolical! Even here in her own room he managed to assert himself.

"You didn't hurt me," she assured David. "I enjoy playing soccer with you. I've told you that many times. Now come over here, the two of you." She held out her arms.

David galloped over, but Daniel held back shyly, his tentative smile making Zen's eyes sting with the memory of her sister. She hugged both boys to her, then told them they could play on her bed while she got dressed.

She watched them for a moment as Daniel pulled out cards and shuffled them dexterously, then dealt the deck for crazy eights, which he had taught David. Soon they were completely absorbed in the game.

In her dressing room, Zen put on the straight, long, cream-colored skirt she had selected. With it she wore a lightweight sea-green wool sweater and medium-heeled pumps of sea-green kid. She chose a seed-pearl anklet, pearl drop earrings, and the pearl pinkie ring that had belonged to her mother.

"I'm almost ready," Zen called to the boys as she entered the bedroom, checking to see that the posts on her earrings were tight.

She stopped in midstream when she saw Damon seated on her chaise longue, his shoeless feet propped up on the ottoman, her jewelry box in his lap. "Where are your shoes? Where are the boys? And what are you doing with my jewel case?" she demanded, wishing her voice were stronger.

Damon pointed to the door. "My shoes are there. The boys have joined their grandmother downstairs, and I wanted to see if you had any of Eleni's jewelry."

Zen stalked across the room and removed her case from his lap, her anger rising close to the boiling point. "What I have or don't have is none of your—"

"I was thinking about you walking barefoot on this fluffy carpet . . . nice, very nice." Damon crossed his arms on his chest and appraised her thoroughly.

"Stop interrupting. What's nice?" Zen snapped.

"Thinking about you walking barefoot . . . thinking about your naked body spread out on this carpet."

Zen gasped at his audacity. "Isn't your fiancée waiting downstairs?"

"Melissa and I are not formally engaged. I told you that." Damon settled himself more comfortably in the chair.

"Leave my room." Zen pointed haughtily toward the door, but the gesture had little impact on Damon.

"Do you have the pink sapphires that belonged to Eleni?" Damon asked, ignoring her demand.

"I don't have any of Eleni's jewels." Zen spun around and replaced the jewel case on the dresser. At once, she sensed that Damon had left the chaise and come up behind her.

"What do you mean?" he asked close to her ear. "All Eleni's gems belong to you. She had no daughter. Are you saying that her jewelry was never sent to you?"

"Nothing."

"Hmm. I'll ask my mother."

"I'm sure much of what Eleni had belonged to the Aristides family, and your mother would want it to stay in the family."

Damon's dark brows met over his nose, and his expression tightened. "I'm the executor of the estate. I will say who gets what."

Zen was about to respond when the muscle jumping at the corner of his mouth warned her to say nothing. She didn't want to encourage an argument so close to dinnertime.

"Come along. If we're going to join the others for a drink, we should go down now." He took Zen's arm under his, threading his fingers through hers with an intimacy that surprised her. When she tried to pull free, he tightened his hold and urged her toward the door.

"Who?" Zen cleared her throat and tried again. "Who's coming to dinner besides your fiancée?"

"I told you that Melissa and I are not formally engaged." He shot the words at her, making her blink.

"So you did." Damn the man! Again Zen tried to free herself. Again Damon tightened his hold.

"Pythagoras Telos, my mother's old friend from Greece, has been staying in this country for some time now, checking into his widespread business interests here. He will be staying with us for a while, and of course he will be at dinner." Damon paused at the head of the stairs. "According to my mother, Thag, as he prefers to be called, was once a suitor for your mother's hand. He's a rich man with homes in California as well as in Greece and London."

Zen stared at him in surprise. "What are you saying? That this man whom I never heard of was once my mother's boyfriend? How is it I've never heard his name mentioned?" Zen tried to picture a burly, tall Greek standing next to her statuesque mother.

Damon urged her down the stairs without answering her question. "Melissa's aunt, Brenda Waite, will be joining us, as will another of my mother's friends from her school days in England, Maud Wills."

"Delightful gathering," Zen murmured as they reached the last steps, "but shouldn't we hurry just a bit?"

"Hurrying is very bad for the digestion," Damon said, looking down at her with a smile that seemed to illuminate the dim room.

Zen felt as though her insides had turned to custard. She struggled to find something cool and sophisticated to say. "Really?" she managed.

"Yes." He stepped onto the marble foyer, then turned to face her, not letting her take the last step down. They were almost eye to eye, but still Damon was taller. "It's ridiculous for a tall man to be involved with a small woman," he said as if to himself.

"Yes, isn't it?" Zen agreed sarcastically.

"Did I tell you that you look glorious in that outfit?" He bent toward her, his nostrils flaring as he took in her perfume. "Even though you're small, you have the loveliest breasts." His hand wandered around her waist and down her backside. "Not to mention the loveliest derriere I've ever seen."

"Do . . . do you realize that someone could come out of the living room and see us?" Zen's voice was husky.

Damon leaned away from her, his eyes dark and shining. "Why did you leave me?"

Astounded, she stared mutely at him.

"Ah, there you are, Damon," said Sophie, bustling over to them. "I see you've brought Xenobia with you." She hesitated as Damon stepped aside and she caught full view of Zen. "Ah . . . did you design that outfit, Xenobia?"

"I designed the skirt, not the top," she answered, licking suddenly dry lips.

"I see." Sophie looked from her son to Zen. "Well, come along. We mustn't keep dear Lissa waiting."

Zen glanced suspiciously at Sophie but could read nothing in her expression. She nodded and came down the last step, trying to move away from Damon. But he stayed close to her, so that they entered the living room side by side.

Zen paused on the threshold and said a silent prayer of thanks because for once the boys were quiet. They were playing cards on the coffee table.

From the settee rose one of the most perfectly groomed women Zen had ever seen. Her black hair was caught in a bun, and a small smile was fixed on her patrician features. She and Damon were the tallest people in the room, making Zen wonder for a moment who the short, dapper man with black hair was.

"Pythagoras Telos," Damon whispered at her side.

"It can't be," Zen whispered back, trying to keep her smile in place as she moved forward. "You said he was once a boyfriend of my mother's. Mother must have been a foot taller than this man."

Damon chuckled. "Thag Telos is a man of great personality."

"Indeed," Zen managed.

Damon moved from Zen's side toward the brunette vision. "Lissa, this is Xenobia Driscoll, Daniel and David's aunt. Zen, this is Melissa Harewell."

"How do you do, Miss Harewell." Zen held out her hand and felt the cool smoothness of Lissa's soft grip.

"How do you do, Xenobia," Lissa replied in carefully modulated tones. "Dear Mrs. Aristides has told me so much about you that I feel I know you already."

"And you haven't armed yourself?" Zen smiled to soften her words and reached for a glass of champagne from a nearby tray.

"Pardon me?" Lissa's deep blue eyes widened in perplexity.

Sophie didn't look up from her position behind the silver tray of canapés where she was alternately feeding the boys and asking them questions about the card game.

"Zen," Damon warned. He walked to Lissa's side and kissed the cheek she proffered. "Zen loves to joke," he explained.

"Yes, she does," David surprised everyone by interjecting. "Once Seamus had a party where everyone had to dress like people from books." He paused to beam at his interested grandmother, his uncle, and the other adults. Knowing what was coming, Zen wanted to drop through the floor. "I was Grumpy," David explained, "one of the Seven Dwarfs. Aunt Zeno was Lady Godawful."

"Does he mean Lady Godiva?" Lissa inquired politely.

"I believe he does," Sophie replied smiling. "Ah . . . it's good for a child to be grounded in the classics."

"Mother," Damon snarled, staring at Zen, a gray cast to his features making them look as though they'd been sculpted in concrete. Anger radiated from every line of his taut body.

"I wore a body stocking," Zen mumbled, not looking at Damon, though she could feel his eyes burning into her.

"Are you ill, Damon?" Lissa asked kindly.

"Sick, yes." His eyes were still riveted on Zen. "You went to a party like that?" He seemed to be grinding out each syllable.

"Isn't it diverting?" Lissa said with pleasure. "Where did you get the horse?"

"Aunt Zeno whitewashed the donkey that Mr. Morphy uses to pull his knife-grinder's cart," David announced clearly.

"How fitting!" Damon growled. "An ass on an ass."

Lissa tittered. "Oh, Damon, you have such a sense of humor."

Zen's hand closed tightly around her glass. "Yes, doesn't he?"

"I do feel, Xenobia, that there is much you could learn about mothering a child," Lissa said. "How to set a good example, to begin with." She smiled.

Zen ground her teeth.

"And," the redoubtable Lissa continued, "I highly disapprove of cardplaying. Cards teach children to gamble."

Zen drew herself up to her full five feet two inches, prepared to do battle for her twins. "Cardplaying is an excellent way to teach a youngster mathematics."

"How droll." Lissa sighed, her doelike eyes shifting to Damon. "No one denies that the Irish are droll, but poor David needs help with pronunciation. I'm sure I can help with that, and with his arithmetic."

"I'll have you know that people in some sections of Ireland are said to make the most perfect use of the English language." Zen took a deep breath. "And you know what you can do with—"

"I think dinner is being served." Damon stepped forward and took Lissa's arm, turning her toward the door.

"Come, boys," Sophie said. She sailed screnely out of the room, the boys and other guests trailing after her, leaving a seething Zen standing furious and alone.

Chapter 3

DINNER DID NOT go well for Zen. If the boys hadn't been there, she would have left the table. She found it most difficult to listen as Lissa continued to explain how to raise two boys who, unfortunately, happened to be twins.

"Of course, everyone knows that one twin is always dominant." Lissa sighed as she looked at David and Daniel, who smiled back at her, then continued eating. "It would be a happier situation if Daniel were the dominant one, even though neither boy seems to have the superior intelligence of my nephew Leonard."

"Now just a minute..." Zen struggled to control her temper.

"The boys do as well as their father and uncle did at this age, perhaps a little better." Sophie hastened to interject, smiling at Lissa.

Zen took a forkful of moussaka and gasped as the hot food burned her mouth. She grabbed her water glass and took long swallows.

"They seem to have strange eating habits in Ireland, too," Lissa mused.

"I like Ireland." David scowled. "Robbie lives there."

"Of course, dear. We all like primitive places until we are older."

"We do?" David looked puzzled, then glanced at his aunt. "Why is your face so red, Aunt Zeno? Is the food burning your mouth again?"

"Something is burning me." Zen glared.

When Lona came for the boys a few minutes later, Zen excused herself. "I always tell David and Daniel a story before bedtime," she explained.

"That's a good practice when they are very young," Lissa pronounced brightly, but she held up a cautioning finger. "I do think, however, that at this age, when they are almost ready for boarding school—"

"They are seven years old!" Zen expostulated.

"Ah...true...but the sooner they have a strong scholastic environment—"

"I'll see you in—"

"I think it well for you to see to the boys," Pythagoras Telos interrupted. He had been silent during most of dinner, but now he took Zen's arm in a surprisingly strong clasp and led her into the hall, where he gave her a courtly bow, his eyes following after the twins as they and Lona went up the stairs. "How my Maria would have loved those boys," he said softly.

"My mother?" Zen whispered, feeling much subdued.

"Yes, your mother. I loved her dearly, even after she married Patrick Driscoll." He sighed wistfully.

Zen began to see the older man with new eyes. "My mother was a lucky woman to have two such fine men love her."

Pythagoras Telos regarded her thoughtfully. "You are her child. Oh, not outwardly, but in many ways I see my Maria." He turned on one well-shod foot and returned to the dining room.

Zen went upstairs and changed into jeans and a cotton shirt. Bathing the twins was like an Olympic competition to see who would get wetter—the boys, Lona, or herself. But Zen delighted in the boys' antics.

By the time they were in their beds waiting for their uncle and grandmother to come and say good night, Zen was glad to escape to her room and change again, into dry clothes. Feeling restless, she chose dove gray sweat pants and a sweat shirt. She would jog around the yard before going to bed.

When she stepped outside, she saw that Damon's car was missing. She guessed that he had taken Melissa Harewell home.

The night was so beautiful with the moon rising over the water. Zen paused to admire the scene, then climbed the rickety steps of a gazebo built on a point of land near the water.

Weeds and bracken surrounded the building, whose disrepair contrasted sharply with the well-tended main house and grounds.

Zen welcomed the feeling of solitude and neglect. She was reminded of her untenable position in the Aristides household. She would never give the twins over to the manicured, repressive hands of Melissa Harewell. Boarding school for David and Daniel? Never! She would see Damon in hell first!

"So this is where you are." The deep voice of the man she'd been thinking about, coming out of the pitch darkness, shocked her out of her reverie and made her jump in surprise.

She whirled to face him and stumbled into a network of cobwebs. "Aaagh! Oh, I hate this stuff. It's in my mouth, my eyebrows. Damn you, Damon, must you move like a fox?" She flailed her hands in a futile attempt to escape the sticky webs.

"Here, let me help you." Damon vaulted over the railing with ease and pulled Zen into his arms. He wiped the sticky silk from her face and form with a handkerchief he pulled from his pocket. "There, is that better?"

She nodded. "Yes, thank you, most of it's gone. That's one of the things I hated most about camping—cobwebs... and burdocks. I always had them on my clothes.

The more I picked them off, the more they got stuck on me."

"I hated the mosquitoes and the blackflies," Damon said.

"Blackflies!" Zen exclaimed, closing her eyes. "I'd forgotten about them. Daddy used to take us to his cabin on Tupper Lake in the Adirondacks, and he would paint, not seeming to notice when the blackflies started to swarm around him. How they stung!"

"And the deerflies," Damon added.

"Yes! Oh, those horrid flies that would follow when you went to the farm for milk and eggs. Eleni would scream bloody murder. She always hated them worst of all." Zen started to laugh, not even noticing when her laughter turned to sobs. Her return to Long Island had forced her to recall painful memories she'd gone to Ireland to forget.

Damon drew her gently into his arms, caressing her hair and back. "You still miss her, don't you?" he said softly.

Zen gulped and nodded, hardly realizing that her face was pressed against his chest. "It was so awful losing her so soon after my mother and father. If it hadn't been for David, I . . . I don't know what I would have done."

"But why couldn't you turn to me?" Damon whispered in an anguished voice, running his hands up and down her arms in a tender message.

Zen looked up, aware all at once of how her blood seemed to be pounding out of rhythm. She tried to push away from him. "No, I couldn't do that." She gasped for air, feeling as though she had just climbed a mountain, trying to ignore the warmth of his closeness.

"Zen, listen to me. I know you hated what Lissa said tonight about sending the boys to boarding school."

"Never."

"Will you listen?" Damon's voice, harsh all at once, caught Zen's full attention. "You don't have to do anything you don't want to do with either David or Daniel.

You can decide how the boys are raised. You can be their mother."

She looked at him without understanding.

"Marry me . . . and you'll have both boys," Damon said in a choked whisper.

Be Damon's wife? Be with him always?

For another moment Zen didn't move—hope, fear, delight, and desire all whirling inside her. Then fury erupted. "And what will you do with your other wife, Melissa? Put her on hold? Or will you put me on hold and tend her? No, damn you, no!"

Finding strength she didn't know she possessed, Zen pushed Damon, catching him off guard. He staggered backward, trying to maintain his balance. When he hit the railing, it looked as if he would regain his footing. But the rotted wood of the gazebo gave way with a tearing crash, sending Damon and the railing down into the shrubbery.

Zen stood aghast as he began thrashing in the bushes, trying to stand up. "Oh, my God! How did that happen? I'm sorry, Damon. What have I done!"

Pain and love raging within her, Zen knew she couldn't face Damon's wrath. Feeling like the greatest coward who had ever lived, she turned and ran from him. He called her name over and over again, but she kept running.

She didn't stop until she was in her room. She tore off her clothes and stepped under the shower, lathering her body with vicious strokes that reddened her skin. "What the blazes does he think he's doing?" she demanded out loud as she stood at the mirror minutes later, pulling a comb through her hair. "Setting up an At Home Concubine Bureau, is he? Damn him to hell! He won't use me."

Furious, she stalked naked into her bedroom, still mumbling to herself, her body slippery with the lotion she had just rubbed over it.

A knock sounded, and the door swung open. Damon entered. "Zen, if you would just listen to me, calm down—" He saw her and stopped short, one hand raised defensively, bracken still clinging to his clothes. The angry look on his face softened to one of sensual shock as his eyes assessed her.

Zen's temper flared anew. "Get out of here!" Making no move to cover herself, she reached for a figurine on a side table and threw it against the wall with all her might.

The statue grazed the side of Damon's head, making him blink, but he didn't take his eyes off her body. "I'm going," he mumbled, "but this isn't the end of it."

"It damn well better be!" Zen watched the door close, her chin trembling with suppressed emotion. "And what's more, I never used to swear like this in Dublin," she added quietly, sniffing.

Feeling thoroughly dispirited, she pulled on a silk wraparound, slipped on soft silk scuffs, and bent to pick up the pieces of the broken figurine.

A knock on the door sent Zen scrambling for another weapon. But at the sound of the voice coming through the door she sighed with relief. "It is I, Lona, Miss Driscoll. Kyrie Damon sent me to clean up the broken china. He said he broke it by accident."

"He did no such thing." Zen rose from her knees and opened the door, facing Lona with arms akimbo. "I broke it. I threw it at him."

Lona nodded, stonefaced.

"He's an aggravator and an instigator," Zen declared hotly.

"As a boy he was always full of mischief," Lona concurred, sweeping up the broken china.

"Mischief! The man is a...a revolutionary!"

Lona turned on the vacuum cleaner, effectively silencing Zen. Once the rug was clean, she turned off the machine and picked up the plastic bag filled with shards. "Good night, Miss Driscoll," she murmured.

"Good night, Lona."

* * *

Zen didn't sleep well that night. Not even the sweet-smelling sheets soothed her. She tossed and turned until the eastern sky began to lighten.

She rose late in the morning, still disgruntled, feeling lethargic and out of sorts.

She was wrapping a robe around her when her bedroom door crashed open and the boys tumbled in, grinning exuberantly.

"Breakfast time!" David sang out, flinging himself at her. Daniel hung back shyly until Zen pulled him forward. She hugged him fiercely, suddenly overwhelmed with love for them.

Daniel looked up at her, his eyes glinting with mirth. "Lona said we're having pancakes today."

"Are they like the oatcakes Bridie used to make me, Aunt Zeno?" David asked, referring to the woman who had been their housekeeper in the Dublin apartment.

"A little like that, yes," Zen answered. "Why don't you two go downstairs and wait for me in the morning room? Then the three of us can eat together."

"Uncle Damon will be there, too," David told her. "He's staying home today. He's sick . . . but he's eating with us anyway."

Zen paused at the bathroom doorway. "Sick? What's wrong with him?" Her throat tightened.

"He isn't sick, Aunt Zeno. He itches," Daniel explained. Both boys galloped out of the room, leaving Zen with her mouth open, poised to ask another question.

Dismissing her concern, she showered, brushed her teeth, and put on turquoise slacks and a cotton shirt. The slacks were made of a stretchable wool she had designed herself. The shirt was a madras cotton in cream and turquoise. She wore turquoise hand-tooled Turkish slippers.

She went down the stairs wondering if Melissa was coming to breakfast. Was that why Damon was staying home from work? The boys might have assumed he was sick. She geared herself to face the honey-voiced Melissa. Sophie, she was sure, would still be in bed. Mrs.

Aristides rarely rose before eleven o'clock.

As she approached the morning room, Zen heard David's boisterous voice and the quieter responses of his twin.

"Good morning." Expecting to see Lissa, she stretched her mouth into its widest smile. Instead, she saw only Damon. At least he resembled Damon. Zen stared aghast at his red and swollen face. "What happened to you? You look like the Pillsbury Dough Boy."

"Very funny." Damon's mouth was almost lost in his swollen cheeks. "There was poison ivy around the gazebo," he explained.

"Good Lord!" Zen breathed, torn between contrition and amusement.

Damon shot her a warning look. "If you laugh, Xenobia," he said with a calm menace, "I'll toss you in the poison ivy, too."

"Well, you needn't get huffy," she retorted. "It *was* an accident."

He held up one hand. "Don't say that. Ever since you arrived, you've caused one *accident* after another. I'm beginning to wonder if there's something more than that behind the incidents."

Zen put her hands on her hips. "You're not going to sit there and tell me you think I *knew* there was poison ivy..." Catching the boys' solemn gazes, she fell silent. "What I mean is, I'm very sorry you're experiencing...er...such discomfort."

"Thank you," Damon said politely, then winced and began rubbing his back against his chair.

"I don't think you should scratch," Zen said.

"I can't help it," he snapped.

"What's that funny white stuff on your arms, Uncle Damon?" David asked.

"Poison ivy cream," Damon answered tersely.

"Oh." David considered for a moment before adding, "Daniel said that Lona says it will last two weeks. Will it?"

"Maybe." Damon stared at Zen as she struggled to

stifle a giggle. She coughed into her napkin and took a sip of orange juice.

"Aunt Zeno had a very bad rash once," David said thoughtfully.

Oh, no, not that story! "David, I don't think your uncle is interested in hearing about that," Zen suggested nervously.

Damon regarded her with new interest. "Actually, I'd love to hear about it," he assured the boy.

"Well, the doctor told Aunt Zen that if her tests didn't come out right she would have to go to the health place . . . I think. But she didn't, did you, Aunt Zeno?"

"No, dear." Zen smiled with effort as she remembered the awful rash she had picked up . . . and how the doctor had suggested she might have contracted a recurrent illness from recent sexual contact. The doctor had made her so angry by suggesting such a thing that she had shouted imprecations and left in a huff. The doctor had called back two days later with the results of the test— and to apologize. The rash had been caused by an allergic reaction to some untreated fabric.

Damon waited until the boys were playing games with their alphabet cereal before he leaned forward and whispered, "And did the rash come back, Zen?"

"You have a low-class mind," she accused him.

"How much did you pay the medical people to falsify the results of the test?"

She glared at him, furious at his insinuations. It was on the tip of her tongue to say that, if she had contracted such a disease, she must have picked it up from him, the only man with whom she had ever been intimate in her life. But she bit her lip, knowing he wouldn't believe her.

She considered his present mood. Damon was apt to use any excuse to cross swords with her, but he rarely resorted to such crass badinage. The poison ivy must be driving him wild.

Tamping down her temper, she poured herself a cup of coffee.

Later that day she took the boys down to the Sound. Though it was warm for late April, the water was icy cold. David and Daniel skipped stones, trying hard to outshoot Zen and crowing with delight when they succeeded.

"Is that a dog swimming out there, Aunt Zeno?" Daniel pointed to a dark object bobbing on the cold waves.

Zen held up a hand to shade her eyes and stared, then nodded slowly. "Yes . . . and he looks tired. What could he be doing out there in such cold water?"

"Maybe he fell off a ship, Aunt Zeno." David said in awed tones. "C'mon, doggy, c'mon," he shouted. Daniel immediately joined in.

"Boys, we don't know who this dog belongs to. Perhaps a neighbor . . ." Zen's voice trailed off as she watched the animal struggle valiantly against the current. "C'mon, dog, c'mon. You can do it." She looked around for a boat or something with which to help the animal.

"Aunt Zeno, there's a life ring in the boat house that Uncle Damon hangs—"

"Good boy," Zen interrupted Daniel. She hurried to the boat house, calling to the boys to stay where they were.

It took mere minutes for Zen to find the ring hanging on the wall, precious seconds to run back to where David was calling to the dog through his cupped hands, urging it to shore.

Praying she could remember how her father had taught her to throw a ring, Zen began to whirl it over her head in slow circles. She twirled it in wider arcs, then let go. The ring sailed out over the water but fell far short of the dog.

Both boys groaned.

"Try again, Aunt Zeno," David urged anxiously.

"What the hell's going on here?" Damon demanded, coming up behind them. They turned gratefully to him.

Zen vaguely noticed that his poison ivy seemed to be getting worse. "The dog," she panted, pointing out over the water.

Damon followed the direction of her gesture, squinting against the sun. "Poor devil's flagging," he muttered. He grabbed the ring from Zen, coiled the rope, and flung it in a high arc. The ring landed directly in front of the dog. "Damn smart animal," he muttered as the dog lunged at the ring and grasped it with strong jaws. Damon began pulling slowly and steadily, being careful not to swamp the dog and force him to release his hold.

When the dog reached shallow water, Zen rushed forward, but Damon stopped her, pushing the rope into her hands and entering the water himself. He grimaced at the frigid cold.

"He could be dangerous," Damon explained, "even though he looks too tired to be a threat to anyone." As if sensing imminent rescue, the animal fixed hope-filled eyes on him.

The water reached Damon's chest when he was finally able to grab the dog by the neck and pull him close. Moments later, both man and dog reached land safely.

"Will he die, Uncle Damon?" David asked anxiously as the exhausted animal lay on his side, his body heaving.

Zen saw Damon shiver, and her concern deepened. "Damon, you mustn't stay here. You're soaked. I'll take care of the dog. You go inside and change." She gave him a slight push.

"We'll all go back to the house. Leave the ring there, Zen. I'll have Yanos see to it." Damon lifted the dog into his arms and carried him, the boys asking questions and racing around him. Zen trailed behind, muttering to herself. "See if I care if you get pneumonia on top of poison ivy. I suppose you'll blame this on me, too."

"Hurry up, Aunt Zeno. Uncle Damon says we have to get the dog warm." Daniel glanced back at her with a worried frown.

They took the dog to the barnlike building in back of the house where the Aristides automobiles and bicycles were kept. The taciturn Yanos and his wife Maria lived in an apartment on the second floor.

Damon carried the dog to the workroom in the back of the carriage house, where tools of every description hung on the walls. It was a good-sized rectangular room with a potbellied stove set on a brick foundation in the center. "Zen, there are clean drop cloths in that cupboard." Damon nodded toward ceiling-to-floor doors against one wall.

Zen rushed to get the cloths and spread them on the cement floor near the stove, where Damon placed the dog. She began drying the animal with other cloths she found on the shelves. "Damon, go get dressed," she urged.

He nodded. "I'll go take a shower."

The boys helped Zen rub the heavy dog dry.

"Why are his eyes closed?" Daniel asked in hushed tones.

"He's so tired, dear." Zen tried to sound reassuring, but she sensed the dog was in poor shape.

"What's all this?" Yanos asked entering the carriage house. "Kyrie Damon tells me that this creature has come a long way. I will give him some of my herbs, and they will give him strength."

"You will?" both boys chorused, looking at Yanos, their eyes brimming with hope.

"Yes, I will do that. In fact, I will take him to the stable where I keep the tonics for the horses. Soon he will be fine."

It was hours later before Zen was able to convince the boys to return to the house with her. "After all, you've missed your lunch. You must be hungry. Dinner will be in an hour or so. Perhaps we can have some snacks first."

David thrust his jaw out. "I want to take care of the dog. I'll eat down here."

"Me, too," Daniel agreed.

"If you interfere with what Yanos is doing with the dog, he won't have as good a chance of getting well," Zen told them.

Yanos nodded in agreement and assured the boys that they could come down to the barn and visit the dog when they had eaten. Finally they took Zen's hand and went with her to the house.

"He's big, isn't he, Aunt Zeno," Daniel said. "I've

never seen a dog with curly brown hair before."

"I'm not sure, but I think he might be a Chesapeake Bay retriever." Zen paused. "When I was in college I worked for a vet, and he had big charts on the wall with pictures of dogs. This one looks like one of the retrievers."

"I'll call him Curly," David decided.

"I'll call him Curly, too," Daniel echoed.

"The dog may have an owner," Zen warned them, even though she had seen no collar.

Dinner that evening was a noisy affair. The boys related the story of Curly's rescue over and over again, from the salad through the dessert. Since they had already told Sophie and Pythagoras most of the story during the cocktail hour, as they devoured apples and oranges to appease their hunger, Zen was sure Sophie must be growing irritated.

But she replied patiently to all their observations. "I see," she said when the boys told her the dog had no collar.

"He could sleep in the house ... maybe," David offered.

"David," Zen remonstrated.

"In our bedroom," Daniel suggested, beaming.

Damon had the last word. "Let's see if Yanos can make him well first. And then we'll see if he's a good dog, and not a rogue."

"He is a good dog." David scowled.

"Yes, he is," parroted his twin.

"Yanos knows all about animals," Thag commented. "I'm sure he will be able to tell us much about the dog." He smiled at the boys. "Every dog needs a boy, I think."

"No, my friend, every boy needs a dog," Sophie amended.

"Either way is good," David assured his grandmother, making her smile.

Zen looked at Sophie Aristides, stunned by the doting expression on her face as she regarded the twins. Zen cleared her throat to reprimand David for assuming that he could bring the dog into the house, when Sophie surprised her further by saying, "When the dog is well, we will see where in the house he can sleep." She smiled serenely as the boys whooped with glee.

After dinner, Thag and Sophie accompanied the boys to the stable to check on the progress of their patient.

Zen was pleasantly surprised when the huge brown head rose from the bed of cloths and the thick tail wagged once. "He does look better," she whispered to Damon, who was standing next to her.

He nodded. "But I don't think we'll say too much to the boys about keeping him until I run an ad to see if he belongs to someone."

Zen nodded, watching Daniel and David. "No, wait," she admonished them when they tried to mover closer, concerned for their safety.

Yanos appeared with a bottle of dark liquid and a chamois cloth. "I'm going to rub him down with liniment. His muscles must be sore."

The two boys watched with absorbed concentration as Yanos brought the wet cloth down the dog's legs.

"He's a good one, Kyrie." Yanos looked up at Damon. "He knows that I try to help him, and he is still. Even when I give him his food, he lets me touch his dish while he eats. I think the boys can touch him."

"Damon." Zen gripped his arm.

"It's all right, Zen. I'll watch them. Come here, you two." Damon squatted down near the dog's head, talking quietly to the animal, who watched him soulfully, then gazed at David and Daniel as they moved to touch him. The dog's eyes closed once; then he pushed his head at the boys' hands, startling them, making them laugh breathlessly.

"Look at me, Aunt Zen," Daniel called. "Do you want to pet him, too?"

The boys weren't satisfied until both Thag and Sophie had also bent to stroke the dog.

Finally Zen was able to urge them back to the house,

the two of them chattering all the way through the kitchen and up the back stairs to their room.

It was past ten o'clock by the time Zen had returned to her own room and prepared for bed. She intended to read before going to sleep.

A noise out in the hall caught her attention. Thinking the boys might be sneaking outside to see the dog, she opened the door quietly. Seeing nothing, she checked on the boys and found them sleeping. She was on her way back to her room when she noticed that the double doors leading to Damon's suite were open. A light shone from the interior.

She hesitated, but finally decided to go to bed. Then she heard a bump and a muttered imprecation. She paused, peering down the corridor. She knocked and waited. When no one replied, she knocked again, then tiptoed down the hallway and entered a spacious foyer. The living room was on her left and a small office or library on her right. Directly in front of her was a stairway leading to a balcony that overlooked the living room and foyer. She stopped there when she heard more bumping sounds and then a curse. The noise was coming from upstairs.

"Damon? Damon, are you all right?" She stopped at the foot of the stairs, looking up, her hand on the banister.

"Who is it?" he demanded striding from the room onto the balcony, naked except for a towel wrapped around his middle. He scratched with both hands at the reddened welts on his chest.

"Don't itch," Zen said, going up the steps, her eyes riveted on his male form, his breadth of shoulder, the silken ripple of muscle across his chest, the narrow black hair that . . . She shook her head and repeated, "Don't itch."

"I damn well can't help it," Damon barked down at her, scowling fiercely.

"Here," Zen gathered her silk robe in one hand and hurried up the rest of the stairs. She followed him into his room, unable to take her eyes from his back. "Let me put some lotion on you," she offered.

"Not yet. I'm going to take a baking soda bath first. Dammit, this itching is driving me mad." He scratched his shoulders, grimacing at Zen, then disappeared into the bathroom. "The tub will run over," he mumbled.

Zen heard a splash and a groan, then more cursing. She took a deep breath. "Damon, can I help?" Taking her courage in both hands, she walked into the room.

For a moment she was struck mute by the dimly lit interior. "Glory," she breathed. "Trust you to have a real Roman bath. This is the biggest bathroom I've ever seen. Lord, a sauna . . . hot tub . . . whirlpool bath . . . and all in peach-colored tile." Zen stared up at the mirrored ceiling, which hadn't clouded over in the steamy room.

"Salmon color." Damon, lying up to his chest in hot water, opened one eye to glare at her. "Not peach, salmon. Are you color-blind?"

"I'm not color-blind. Are you? God, what a testimonial to old movies." Zen chuckled, then sobered immediately when her eyes fell on Damon. She could see very little of him in the dim light, but just the thought that he was naked left her feeling weak in the knees.

"If you came in my bath just to insult my color scheme . . . owww!" He closed his eyes and began rubbing his back against the smooth tub. "This is torture," he moaned.

As if in a dream, Zen walked forward, pulled up her silk robe, and knelt down on the carpet. She leaned over the rim of the circular tub, which was recessed into the floor. "Turn around and I'll scratch your back for you . . . even though I don't believe—wait! What are you doing? I'll get wet. Ohhh, damn you!"

Damon had caught her under the arms and pulled her, robe and all, into the tub. "Give me poison ivy, will you?" he said. "Then you come up here and laugh at my apartment! Well, how do you like this, my girl?"

"You fool," Zen sputtered. Water tasting of baking soda splashed into her mouth. Her arms and legs became tangled in her robe. "This is silk, Damon. It will be ruined." She flailed wildly at him, but the sodden material hampered her movements.

"Relax and enjoy it, darling," Damon soothed, laughing. "Baking soda is good for your skin."

"I do not have poison ivy." She pushed a clump of wet hair off her face. "I just showered." She spat water from her mouth and sneezed.

"Don't worry." Damon reached up to a shelf near his head and brought down several plastic containers. "All the soap you could need or want...any kind." He grinned at her, seeming to have forgotten his discomfort. "Gotcha," he mumbled, her arms tightening around her and his eyes roving possessively over her.

"What do you mean?" Suspicion warred with reason, and won. "You aren't in pain," she exclaimed. "This was a ruse to get me in here!"

"Well, I was in discomfort—at first anyway."

"You lured me in here," she sputtered, splashing more water into her mouth in an effort to free herself from his iron grip.

"You're so dramatic." Damon chuckled and clamped her to his body.

"You're taking a terrible revenge on me, is that it? Infecting me with your poison ivy?" Zen was furious.

"My physician tells me that, unless people are hyperallergic, they're highly unlikely to get poison ivy except from direct exposure to the plant." Damon bent forward, his tongue coming out to tease the corner of her mouth.

"Your doctor is a quack. Besides, how do you know I'm not one of those hyperallergic people?" Zen arched her neck, trying to get away from him.

Damon lifted her slightly away from him, his eyes burning into hers. "Are you?"

"I...I guess not," she answered.

Damon stared at her for a longer moment, then released her abruptly, pushing her to her feet in the tub but staying seated himself. "I've just decided that I can't take the chance with you." He studied her wet body. The silk robe clung like a second skin. She stared back, baffled, swamped by an illogical disappointment with her sudden freedom. "The thought of all that pinky whiteness becoming red and covered with welts is repellent to me," Damon went on. He closed his eyes. "I think I've finally gone around the bend," he added as though to himself. "Having a lovely woman almost naked beside me and not making love to her! I must be crazy!"

Zen's temper burst. How many women had taken baths with Damon. She wouldn't stay with him a moment longer. Rising to her full height, she lifted the hem of her robe and squeezed it over his head. "How dare you try to give me poison ivy?" she lashed out producing the first argument that came to mind. Then she lifted three bottles of shampoo from the shelf, uncorked them, and dumped the contents on Damon. She threw down the empty containers, grabbed a bath sheet, and stormed out of the room.

"Zen . . . what the hell did you do that for? Damn, the bubbles. What's the matter with you? Come back here. We have to talk. We're getting married."

"I'll see you in hell first," Zen called over her shoulder as she dripped down the stairs to the foyer, the oversized towel trailing after her like a train. "Womanizer. Charlatan." She stomped down the hall. "Svengali." She struggled to suppress the feelings that urged her to rush back to him and throw herself into his arms. Part of her longed to be held by him, yearned to forget the rest of the world. "No . . . no, I won't be part of his harem," she mumbled.

Back in her own bathroom Zen dried herself, and climbed into bed. She tried to sleep, but images of her and Damon making love in the tub kept surfacing in her mind.

Chapter 4

ZEN KEPT A wary eye on Damon for the next two weeks as his poison ivy slowly healed. He stayed home for much of that time but kept in close contact with his New York office. Sometimes Zen took his calls. There was an emergency with Venus Airlines, another with one of his shipping interests. Meetings were called that he must attend. She began to see that Damon Aristides was, indeed, an important industrialist and a shrewd businessman.

One day a man named Desmond came to see Damon. He explained that he was sure the dog they were calling Curly had belonged to a friend whose fishing boat had sunk in the Sound. The man's body had been washed ashore a few days previously.

"That's why I came over today, Mr. Aristides. I thought this might be Jocko, old Jim's dog. The sheriff said Jim had teeth marks in his shoulder, as though the dog had tried to tow him for a while after the boat capsized. Then they surmise the current took them farther out. Old Jim died, and the dog tried to save himself." Mr. Desmond knocked his pipe against the bottom of his shoe, nodding to Zen as she stood listening. He turned to watch Curly cavort with the two boys, fetching the ball they threw for him.

"Jim Enright had no family," he went on, "but kids were always coming around to play with Jocko and get fishing lessons from Jim." He shook his head. "My wife and I will miss him, but you're welcome to keep the dog. We can't take him, and I'd hate to see him put down."

"Thank you, Mr. Desmond." Damon accompanied the man to his car.

Zen saw the man shake his head, but Damon insisted that he take the bills he pressed into his hand.

"You did us a favor by coming, Mr. Desmond, and you and your wife are welcome to come by and visit the dog any time."

Zen waited until the car had disappeared from sight before joining Damon on the lawn. "It was kind of him to come," she said.

Damon turned, regarding her through narrowed lids. "Are you speaking to me again?" His eyes made a lazy survey of her, from her breasts to her ankles.

"Stop doing that . . . and I never stopped speaking to you," Zen said angrily.

"Ah, yes, those poignant phrases like, 'No, I don't care for a roll, thank you,' and 'Yes, the weather is fine,'" Damon touched a finger to her lips. "We're getting married."

"What about Melissa?" Zen's mouth felt dry as hope and despair warred within her. Tell me you love me, damn you, she pleaded silently.

"Melissa and I have had a long talk. We've decided we don't suit. She has interests elsewhere."

Suddenly Zen felt as light as air. Happiness bubbled up inside her, followed swiftly by horror. Had she lost complete control of her emotions? She glanced at Damon briefly, then away. "Will that happen to me after a while? Will we talk, then decide we don't suit?" She swallowed past the lump in her throat, fearing she had exposed too much of her feelings to him.

"No," Damon answered tersely.

She tried to find words to prove that she was as cool as he was. "The boys want me to see Curly's new trick," she said, heading across the lawn. But, to her dismay, Damon's long strides kept easy pace with hers.

Daniel ran to meet them. "Aunt Zeno, Curly can catch the ball and bring it back to us." His bright smile made Zen's heart turn over with love.

"Is that the trick you were going to show me?" she asked.

"Not exactly," David said, coming up to them, a panting Curly at his side. The dog dwarfed both boys, yet he was so gentle and playful that Zen's initial worry had all but vanished. "C'mon, Uncle Damon, you come, too. We want to show you something." David looked up at his uncle. "I know it hurt to have poison ivy, but I liked it when you were home all the time, not just on Saturday." Running after his twin and the dog toward the stable, David didn't see his uncle's face flush with embarrassed pleasure.

Zen knew Damon was deeply touched by what David had said. He'd spent his first days at home constantly on the phone discussing his fishing boats on the West Coast, his computer stores in the Chicago area, his consulting firms in New York, and the airline based in Athens. But the boys had vied for his attention at every turn. More and more, Damon had given in to them. Zen sensed that he felt very close to the twins.

He opened his mouth to say something, then changed his mind, and instead took Zen's arm and followed the boys to the stable in silence.

The sudden darkness of the interior momentarily blinded them. They called out to David.

"Up here, Uncle Damon," he shouted. "Up in the loft."

"I thought I told you not to climb up there unless Yanos was with you," Zen scolded. She stepped purposefully over the ladder and began to climb, stopping when she was able to rest both arms on the floor of the loft and see where the boys were huddled in a corner. Pushing away a little, she shook her finger at them and took a deep breath to berate them—then unexpectedly lost her balance. She grabbed frantically for a handhold, knocking some loose hay off the shelf.

"Zen, for God's sake! Are you trying to bury me in hay?"

She looked over her shoulder down at Damon, who was picking pieces of straw off himself and shaking his head ruefully. "I didn't drop much hay," she replied.

"No? I'm just glad the pitchfork was down here."

"Very funny."

"Aunt Zeno, will you come over here?" Daniel called impatiently. "Look."

Zen hesitated. She wasn't fond of heights and she didn't relish climbing back down once she was up there. But both boys were calling for her. "Oh, all right. I'll be right down, Damon." She climbed the rest of the way into the loft and went over to the boys.

David pointed to a patient mama cat suckling four kittens. "Aren't they nice? Yanos said we're not to touch them for a few days yet." His voice dropped to a whisper. "Aren't they small?"

"Yes, they are." Zen sat cross-legged in the hay and listened to the faint mewing of the tiny creatures.

"I hope Curly doesn't try to come up here," David said.

"I'm sure he's smarter than that," Damon answered as he dropped down next to Zen and smiled at the boys. "So, you're a mother, are you, Zaza?" He reached out and petted the silver tabby. She pushed her head against his hand. "She's a very good mother, too."

As the boys sat entranced, Damon told them stories about other animals on the estate. Zen leaned comfortably against a bale of hay, unable to take her eyes off Damon. Her heart thudded as she studied his dark head and broad shoulders. When he reached out to tousle David's head with a large hand, her face flushed with warmth. He seemed to radiate a sense of care and protection, and deep inside she yearned to have him touch her in the same familiar way. But in her imagination his touch soon turned hot and possessive ... She shifted restlessly and lowered her eyes.

When they climbed down from the loft some time later, Damon went first, Daniel and David following. Zen took a deep breath, slid over the edge on her stomach, and felt for a rung. An iron hand grasped her ankle and positioned her foot on it.

"There, you're set now, darling. Just come ahead. I'm here." Damon's voice seemed to vibrate through her. She felt his body behind hers as they descended the rest of the way together.

Once on the ground, she brushed the straw from her clothes and watched the boys as they talked to Yanos, the horses, and the dog. She looked up at Damon. "How did you know I was leery about coming down the ladder?"

"I saw the expression in your eyes when you looked down at me." He put an arm around her. "When are you going to admit that it would be better all around if we got married?"

"Better for whom?"

"Better for us. Better for the boys. They need a home with a mother and a father."

"Yes, they do," Zen agreed.

Damon turned her to face him. "Then you'll marry me?"

"Or marry someone else ... Ouch, you're squeezing me!" Zen bit her lip at the fire in his eyes.

"Don't tease me, love." Damon kissed the tip of her nose. "I don't like it. And you'd damn well better know that to get those two boys you'll have to have me, too."

"I want the boys, but I think we should have a ... a trial engagement. No, wait; don't interrupt. I mean that we should have a time when we try to get along with each other, to see if we're compatible."

Damon halted in front of her, his mouth twisting wryly. "What the hell—"

"If we fight on every issue, argue all points, disagree—"

"Be quiet, Zen. I get the picture. But don't you think you're approaching marriage in a very unrealistic way? Married people disagree on many things, but they stay together."

"Not today they don't," Zen shot back. "If it doesn't feel good, get rid of it. If the glow isn't there every day, toss it out the window." She shook her head, making her red-gold curls swing around her face. "No, I want a stable home for the boys . . . or we go back to the status quo."

"Damn you. You would separate those boys again, knowing how much they mean to each other?"

Guilt flooded Zen. What he said was true. The boys would suffer greatly if they were separated again. But they would also suffer if they lived in a home where the husband didn't love the wife, where the husband might choose a different partner after a time . . .

"Stop daydreaming." Damon gave her a little shake, scattering her thoughts. "You're building straw barriers in that damned convoluted mind of yours." His touch softened. "All right, we'll try it your way . . . for a while."

Zen stiffened as his arm went around her waist again. "There's no need—"

"Drop it, Zen." His arm tightened around her as they neared the boys and the romping dog.

"He's a magnificent-looking animal, isn't he?" Zen said, forgetting for a moment that she was angry with Damon.

"Gentle and intelligent, too. The first day he was able to walk, I saw him down at the water's edge, looking out over the Sound. To me it seemed as though he was paying his respects to Jim, the man who owned him. When I spoke to him, he looked at me with the saddest eyes, then followed me back to the house."

"The house," Zen mused, looking up at him. "I feel guilty that the boys coerced your mother into letting them keep the dog inside."

Damon shrugged. "Don't worry. Mother doesn't seem to mind. And the staff likes him."

* * *

That evening everyone gathered in the living room for cocktails, the boys regaling their grandmother with descriptions of Curly's newest trick. Zen was surprised when Damon stood up and called for everyone's attention.

"I have had Maria bring champagne to us this evening because I have an announcement to make." Zen's face flamed as she anticipated what he was about to say. Damon lifted the bottle from the ice bucket and opened it, pouring the sparkling wine into tulip-shaped glasses and nodding to Maria and Lona to pass them around. "As you know, it is the custom among Greek people for engaged couples to feed each other." Damon now had the full attention of everyone in the room. He turned to a slack-jawed Zen and held his glass to her lips. "Taste, darling. It's Dom Perignon." He laughed when she sipped without thinking. "Xenobia and I will be getting married soon," he added casually.

As everyone applauded and wished them happy, Zen whispered furiously to Damon, "You should have told me you were planning this." She gulped and coughed as bubbles went up her nose.

"And you would have gone along with me? I thought not," Damon answered with a chuckle. He bent to kiss her on the mouth as though they were alone in the room.

"And what of Melissa?" Sophie asked sternly, her hands folded in front of her, refusing to take a glass from Maria until she had heard Damon's answer.

"I've spoken to Melissa," her son said in frosty tones.

"And what of the two families? Was there not an understanding?" his mother persisted.

"I have talked to her father and to her uncles. Melissa seems to be quite interested in one of the Rivaldos," Damon said flatly.

"You mean the winery people?" Sophie inquired.

"They are fine people," Thag interjected. "Dominic Rivaldo has been my friend since we fought in the British commandos together."

"Isn't Rivaldo an Italian name?" Zen asked, hoping to change the subject.

"Yes. We both left our own countries and went to Britain, where we were trained in guerrilla warfare." Thag smiled in rememberance. "We blew up a few bridges in our time."

"How fascinating," Zen said.

"I want to know more of this," Sophie pursued, reluctantly accepting a glass from the hovering Lona, watching like a hawk as the woman poured white grape juice for the boys.

"Zen and I think the boys will be happier if we marry and keep them together," Damon added.

Zen shifted restlessly at the sight of Sophie's unreadable expression. "We haven't ironed out all the details yet," she said nervously, "but the alternative is to split the boys."

"No," David and Daniel chorused.

Daniel came up to Zen and caught her around the leg. "I want to be with you all the time, Aunt Zeno."

She bent over him, holding him. "I want that, too."

"Then it's settled, I suppose," Sophie said, surprising Zen once again. The older woman lifted her glass. "To my son and his bride-to-be." She sipped the champagne, her face inscrutable.

"To Xenobia," Thag toasted, tapping his glass against the boy's juice glasses, delighting them.

Zen's smile was tight as she edged closer to Sophie and whispered, "We aren't planning to marry right away."

"Really? That does surprise me. My son is a very virile man." Zen choked on her champagne and Sophie patted her on the back, then rose and announced dinner. "Come, boys. You will sit next to me this evening. Aunt Xenobia will want to sit next to Uncle Damon." She stared at her son. "And why does she not have a ring?" she demanded.

"Mother," Damon said, irritated, "as it happens, I was going to give Zen a ring this evening."

"You were?" Zen said, stupefied. "When did you get a ring?"

"Don't you want a ring, Aunt Zeno?" David asked.

"No . . . yes, of course." She clenched her fists and followed the boys into the dining room.

Once David and Daniel had wriggled into their chairs, sitting atop pillows that raised them to a comfortable height, David beamed at her. "Uncle Damon is going to show us how to play lacrosse after dinner. Would you like to come, Aunt Zeno?"

"Yes, dear," she said, then frowned, catching Damon's eye. "Isn't that a dangerous sport?"

"All sports can be dangerous. Do you want to coddle the boys?"

"No, but—"

"There you are, then."

Damon was at his most scintillating during dinner, but Zen's temper rose as he constantly turned aside all her efforts to explain that theirs was a trial engagement.

Nevertheless, she was flabbergasted at the tender attention he showed her. When he reached out to grasp her wrist, intercepting a forkful of food on its way to her mouth and indicating that she was to feed it to him, she thought he was joking.

"Feed him, Zen," Thag urged. "It is an old Greek custom among sweethearts that they feed each other at the table."

"Oh." Her eyes met Damon's as he moved her hand up to his mouth, holding the fork there for long seconds—in what Zen thought was a very suggestive way and inappropriate in front of the boys. What would Sophie say?

But when she risked a glance, the older woman looked utterly serene.

"I think I will have a reception so that the rest of the family can meet Xenobia," she announced, after swallowing a bit of fish.

"Like the one you had for Eleni?" Zen asked, remembering the hordes of people who had milled around the house and grounds, bringing expensive gifts. "I don't think—" Zen began.

"That's a good idea, Mother," Damon interrupted, leaning over and kissing Zen's mouth. "You had a bit of parsley there."

"Did not." Zen glanced at the boys, who smiled back at her.

After dinner she accompanied them out to the darkened lawn, where a cool breeze was blowing off the Sound. Yanos threw a switch, and the front lawn was illuminated.

Zen knew little about lacrosse. She didn't understand the scoring, and the object of throwing the ball from nets affixed to poles completely eluded her.

"You do it, Aunt Zeno," David urged, dragging a stick that was far too big for him over to his aunt.

Zen accepted the long pole with the net at the end. When Daniel pitched the ball to her, she swung the pole like a baseball bat.

"No, not that way. Let me show you." Damon approached her as Daniel threw the ball again. Zen swung. "Oww! Dammit, Zen, my face. What are you trying to do, kill me?" Damon held his right cheek, glaring at Zen out of one eye.

"You know," David mused, "Aunt Zeno used to play games better when we lived in Dublin."

"Oh?" Daniel looked from his aunt to his uncle, his lips pursed in thoughtful concentration. "Nonna says that when she travels she never drinks the water. Maybe Aunt Zeno shouldn't drink the water."

Despite his discomfort, Damon laughed and called to Yanos to collect the sticks before he led the boys and Zen back into the house.

"What did Xenobia do now?" Sophie quizzed, earning a glare from Zen.

"How did you know, Nonna?" David climbed up on the settee next to her. Daniel sat cross-legged on the floor.

"She just guessed," Damon answered, even as his mother was opening her mouth to speak.

Conversation centered on lacrosse until the boys went

to bed. Then talk became general. Zen tried to get Damon alone to discuss breaking their trial engagement before things went too far, but he avoided her.

That night Zen sat at her vanity table brushing her hair for a long time. "I can't marry him. He makes me clumsy," she murmured. "I'd kill him in six months."

For some reason she suddenly remembered one of her favorite poems: "The Rime of the Ancient Mariner." She quoted it aloud:

> "God save thee, ancient Mariner!
> From the fiends, that plague thee thus!—
> Why look'st thou so?"—With my crossbow
> I shot the ALBATROSS.

Damn the man, Zen thought, he is my albatross. Not a good omen but a bad omen... "Ohh!" Zen held her head. "I'm totally nuts around that man."

She raised her head and stared at herself in the mirror. I have to get away for a while. Daddy's place at Tupper Lake would be good, just to get things in perspective. I'm afraid to accept Damon into my life. It frightens me to think that he may be the key to all my happiness, to fulfilling all my needs, to helping me appreciate all that's beautiful on this planet. She scowled into the mirror.

All night she tossed and turned, thinking of Damon and her father's cabin in the Adirondack Mountains.

The next day Damon went to his office in Manhattan. There was a bruise on his cheek, but no one mentioned it at the breakfast table. Afterward, David and Daniel took Curly out for his morning run. Thag sauntered after them, leaving Zen and Sophie alone.

"Mrs. Aristides," Zen began, "I've been thinking of taking the boys on an outing, perhaps a trip."

Sophie's eyes narrowed. "To Ireland?"

"Oh, no, not so far. I thought somewhere not far from here ... for just a few days. My father had a cottage in the Adirondacks in a remote section on Tupper Lake. I'd like to take them there for just two days. I wouldn't keep them from you. I give you my word."

Sophie scrutinized her for long moments. "You will need at least a week to sort out your feelings for Damon, but whatever you decide, Xenobia, I must tell you that I have been happy with my grandsons and do not want to give one of them up or separate them."

"I understand." Zen swallowed. "Do you mind if I leave this morning? With Damon leaving for California this afternoon—"

"And he won't be back for several days," Sophie finished, her eyes shining. "My son can be overwhelming at times. I understand your need to be alone with the boys to think."

Zen smiled with relief. "We could take the dog. He'd be good protection."

"And will this place be in adequate condition for you?" Sophie inquired.

Zen considered. "I'll call Terry Watts. He was my father's lawyer, and he'll know if the place is still standing."

Sophie nodded, then lifted a hand to keep her from leaving. "Remember, my son is very aggressive, and I am sure he will find out where you've gone. You will have some days to yourself, though."

Zen's eyes filled with tears of gratitude. "Thank you for trusting and supporting me."

"Hurry along, child. I will have Lona help you."

Their preparations proceeded swiftly. The boys were delighted to be making a trip with Curly.

Yanos checked the Cherokee van and filled the gas tank. Then he gave Zen a few quick instructions on how to drive the cumbersome vehicle. She felt confident that she could handle it.

She was relieved to hear from Terry Watts that the taxes had been paid on the cabin in her name with money remaining from her father's estate, and that as far as he knew the pump, pipes, and appliances had passed their annual inspection by a man hired to check on several pieces of property in the area.

Yanos packed sleeping bags, warm clothing, bug repellent, a first-aid kit, a tent, and all the other sundries he considered necessary into a carrier on top of the Cherokee. Zen belted the boys into the back seat and allowed Curly to run free in the roomy compartment far in the back that could double as sleeping quarters in a pinch.

Calling on all the patience she could muster, Zen drove through heavy traffic to the thruway heading northwest. Once they were speeding away from New York City, she was able to relax somewhat. Riding high in the cab of the Cherokee, she felt as if she were driving a truck.

The boys played endless games of crazy eights while Curly watched them over the back of the seat.

Several hours later, near Albany, she swung onto the Northway, Highway 87, which would take them to the Adirondack region, the mountainous area that covered hundreds of square miles in the northeastern section of the state.

They stopped for lunch at a rest area. Both the boys and Curly loved their double hamburgers with ketchup, onions, and relish.

"I don't think a dog should eat condiments," Zen mumbled.

"Curly likes it, Aunt Zeno," Daniel assured her as he very carefully fed the dog a chocolate milk shake. "Curly isn't fussy."

"Hum," Zen said skeptically.

After they'd finished, the boys disappeared into the men's room while Zen walked Curly on his new leash until he did what he was supposed to, and she cleaned up after him.

Back on the road, the boys' incessant chatter gradually ceased. Zen glanced in the rearview mirror to see that they were both asleep. Curly, too, had his eyes closed, his chin resting on the back of the seat. Zen pushed in a stereo cartridge and played soft music. The traffic thinned out and stretches between towns lengthened after she left the Northway and headed northwest toward Tupper Lake. Soon the road began to twist and turn as they climbed into the mountains.

Zen breathed in the heady spring fragrances of wet evergreens, mossy earth, and sweet wild flowers.

About an hour later the boys woke up as Zen pulled in to a gas station. The attendant, a grizzled man chewing on the stem of his pipe, sauntered over to them. "Fill it, please, but don't top the tank," Zen instructed. "Check the oil too, please."

"Yep...and I'll wash the windshield, too." The man grinned at her around the pipe.

Memory washed over Zen as she recalled other days in the north country and the friendly interest of the people there. "Thank you." She smiled at the man, looking past him to the station.

"Name's Harley." He pointed to the sign on the glass window that said HARLEY'S GARAGE. "Ever'body just calls me Harley."

Zen paid Harley and thanked him.

"Where ya headed?" he inquired, leaning on the door of the Cherokee.

"Our camp on Tupper Lake, called Driscoll's Pineview. Do you know it? It's near Mission."

"Yep, I know Mission. One church, a store, two houses, and a gas station. Your place must be on the side of the hill back in the woody section. Kinda lonely up there. Good to have a dog. Get your food at Dina Lipp's place. Fresh stuff." He nodded and saluted them with two fingers as they pulled away.

The boys were growing tired and restless now. They squirmed in their seats and demanded that they be allowed to unbuckle their seat belts.

"No," Zen told them. "We'll be there soon, but the road to the camp is very bumpy...at least it used to be...and I don't want you bouncing around inside the car. Besides, it's against the law for young children to ride in a car without seat belts. Do you want me to break the law?"

"No, Aunt Zeno." David sighed. "But my bottom hurts."

On the last leg of the trip the boys tried Zen's patience to the limits as she struggled to maneuver the large vehicle down the circuitous road that led from the highway past Tupper Lake.

They entered the hamlet of Mission and turned onto a side road filled with mud and deep ruts. The spring thaw must be worse than usual, Zen surmised, her hands locked on the wheel as the van bucked and skidded down the road. She said a silent prayer of thanks for the four-wheel drive.

They rounded a curve in the muddy road and the lake came into view. A sign read: Driscoll's Pineview Lodge. Heaving a big sigh, she pulled the van to a stop. "We're here, boys. Now, be still. I'm not sure I can make it up the driveway to the cottage."

Zen opened the door of the van and stepped down, studying the winding track that led uphill to a log cabin nestled among the pines. For some reason it looked smaller than Zen remembered. She walked up the rutted track, her heart sinking as she saw the sagging shutters and the holes in the porch screens. It was obvious that no extra care had been given to Pineview Lodge in many years. "Only the taxes have been paid," she said ruefully, deciding to chance the upgrade with the four-wheel-drive vehicle.

She returned to the Cherokee, got behind the wheel, and backed it up to give herself a better start. She drove carefully, and they made it to the top of the incline without incident.

The boys clamored to get out. Curly jumped over the seat and galloped after them. They turned to look at Zen, the boys' faces alight with glee, the dog wagging his tail, his tongue hanging out. Neither of the boys seemed to notice the shabby exterior of the cabin, but Zen dreaded what she would find inside.

"Boys, we may sleep in the van tonight. There will be so much cleaning to do in the—"

"We'll help, Aunt Zeno," David assured her.

Daniel nodded, his eyes bright with enthusiasm.

Smiling, Zen put her apprehension aside as she reached above the door frame for the key that they'd always kept there. "Ah . . . here it is. A little dirty but . . ." She pushed the key into the lock. The door squeaked as it opened. "It ain't much, Ma, but it's home," she said as the musty, dusty interior met her eyes. She reached out to wipe away a cobweb.

"Is it spooky, Aunt Zeno?" David whispered.

"No, but it *is* filthy. Tomorrow we'll have to work hard to get it in shape. Tonight I'll see if we can get the water working. Then I'll clean the bathroom, and you boys can have a shower. We'll eat in the van, from the ice chest."

"That will be fun," Daniel said, looking up the narrow stairway. "What's up there, Aunt Zeno?" he asked, pointing to the spacious loft.

"The bedroom I shared with your mother. There's also a bathroom with a sink and toilet. But the only shower is down here."

Zen went to the power box and threw the switches, praying that the circuit breakers were in good working order. Lights came on, and she sighed with relief, then went to inspect the old refrigerator. "It works," she shouted to the boys, more relieved than she cared to admit when she heard the pump kick in, telling her that water was being pumped from the deep well her father had had dug when he'd built the cabin. She checked the water heater and discovered that it worked too.

"So far everything is on, boys."

To her delight, the boys insisted on helping her scrub the shower stall and tiles. Then they wiped out the small sink and around the toilet. Zen finished by washing the floor and bringing in fresh towels from the camper while the boys took a shower together, she listened to their laughter with pleasure and plugged in the electric heaters. Tomorrow she would check the fireplace flue.

When the boys were finished, Zen took a shower and put on fresh jeans and a shirt.

They ate sandwiches and drank hot tea from one thermos, milk from another. Zen was glad there were few dishes. She was so tired she just rinsed them and left them in the sink.

She released the back seat of the Cherokee to make

a larger area in which to spread the sleeping bags and air mattresses. Curly opted to sleep on the ground outside, his presence giving Zen a feeling of well-being as total darkness descended.

Zen slept restlessly. Damon intruded into her thoughts and dreams. She muttered to herself, punching the pillow, then gazing out the window at the stars. She remembered the young woman who had given herself to Damon Aristides without reserve and knew that she could no longer ignore her still burning feelings for him.

She wanted him. She needed him to complete her life.

She rolled over, sleep claiming her at last.

The next morning was frosty cold, and they shivered in the van.

"You two stay here while I get the cabin warm. Then I'll call you for breakfast."

"Can't, Aunt Zeno. I have to go to the bathroom," Daniel said solemnly.

"Me, too," David agreed.

"All right." Zen laughed at them. "I'll turn on the electric heater in the bathroom. That will warm you up."

The boys scampered out of the camper in robes and slippers, followed by Curly, who didn't seem to notice the cold.

They laughed and joked over breakfast as cereal and eggs disappeared from plates, along with the toast, jam, and milk. Curly devoured two giant dog biscuits in seconds.

The boys surprised Zen by offering to help clean up the cabin. She laughed sometime later when she heard them yelling at Curly to get off the tile floor they had just washed.

Later, Zen found two small braided rugs stored in a closet. After she and the boys had hung them outside on a clothesline and beaten them clean, she arranged them in front of the stone fireplace.

That afternoon they explored the lakeshore. Though Zen warned the boys not to venture onto the wooden dock, which was missing several slats, she felt sure the structure was essentially sound.

"Aunt Zeno, look at Curly." David pointed excitedly as the retriever hurled himself into the water to retrieve a stick. "He's not afraid of the water."

"He was bred to the water, darling. Not even his awful experience would dim his natural inclination to it." The three of them took turns tossing the stick to the dog, who seemed never to tire of the game.

"He gets dry right away, I think." Daniel watched as his pet shook himself.

"Retrievers have an undercoat that protects them from the water so that they can resist both the wet and the cold," Zen told them.

That night, after driving to Dina Lipp's store for supplies, Zen cooked fresh fish and vegetables on the grill. Steamed in foil and seasoned with black pepper and butter, the vegetables were delicious. The fish, broiled with fresh lemon slices and butter, tasted moist and succulent. Both boys ate heartily, then sat in front of the fire watching the flames flicker over the logs.

Zen glanced around the cozy cabin, admiring the results of their hard work. Tonight they would sleep in the front room on air mattresses. Tomorrow they would clean the downstairs bedroom and perhaps start on the loft.

Zen barely had time to make up their beds before both boys fell asleep. Curly lay down next to the front door.

Zen checked the doors, placed a screen in front of the banked fire, turned off the lights, and bedded down next to the boys. But when she closed her eyes, she saw Damon gazing at her, coming toward her, overwhelming her, seeming to swallow her up.

Chapter 5

THREE DAYS PASSED. A bright sun made it warm enough to wear only short-sleeved shirts and slacks during the day, but the nights were cool and they huddled in their sleeping bags dressed in flannel pajamas.

The boys enjoyed working and happily scrubbed floors while Zen washed walls and ceilings.

On the fourth morning Zen was lying in the downstairs bedroom watching the play of sunlight on the pines outside her window, listening to the boys giggling upstairs in the loft. Suddenly Curly began barking and bounded down the stairs. He stood in front of the door, growling.

Just then Zen heard the squeal of brakes, followed by heavy footsteps. Someone knocked loudly on the front door. Her heart pounding, she swung her legs out of bed, snatched up her woolly robe, and stood swaying with surprise as Damon shouted through the door.

"Damn it, Curly, stop that growling. Zen, open this door."

"It's Uncle Damon, it's Uncle Damon," both boys

yelled, half tumbling down the stairs.

"Be careful," Zen called to them. "Isn't that just like him?" she muttered. "Coming on like gang busters, scaring people out of bed. I should tell Curly to bite him." She struggled to pull back the bolt on the front door.

Even as she was turning the handle, Damon burst into the room and lifted her into his arms, leaving her feet dangling above the floor.

"Damn your soul, Xenobia, don't you ever do that to me again." His mouth bore down on hers, his tongue immediately parting her lips. The kiss deepened, his arms tightening as though he would never release her.

"Does this mean you're not really mad at Aunt Zeno, Uncle Damon?" David asked, his eyes wide with curiosity.

Zen was able to separate their mouths by mere centimeters, but she could feel Damon's eyes on her, and his hold didn't ease. "Uncle Damon . . . is just . . . concerned," she gasped, pressing her hands against his shoulders. "Damon . . ."

"That's good. Wanna go fishin'?" David smiled up at them.

"Damon . . ." Zen repeated, digging her nails into his neck.

"Huh? Fishing? Fine . . . but I'm hungry."

"I'll make breakfast," Zen offered. When he didn't move, she whispered. "Put me down."

"What? Oh . . . all right." He let her slide down his body, but a steely arm kept her clamped to his side. Ruefully he rubbed his stubbled chin, noticing the red marks left on Zen's face. "Didn't have time to shave," he muttered. "Drove most of the night, once my mother told me where you were. I had trouble finding the place. I must have driven over most of the Adirondacks before I happened on a gas station that was opening up at five in the morning."

"Harley's?" Daniel asked.

"What? Yes . . . that's the name." Damon yawned.

"Why don't you go to bed?" Zen suggested. "I'll call you when —"

"Aw, we want Uncle Damon to go fishing." David scowled darkly.

Zen was about to respond, but Damon squeezed her waist, stifling another yawn.

"I'll shave, then take the boys fishing. After that I'll go to bed."

Zen nodded, stunned by the burning look in his eyes. She turned to tell the boys, who were already crashing up the stairs, to get dressed and wear boots.

Damon put his hand on her shoulder. "After that, you and I will talk," he said, giving her a lopsided grin.

Once Damon and the boys left to go down to the lake, Zen quickly changed the sheets on her bed so that Damon could sleep there when he came in from fishing.

She couldn't help the happy feeling welling up inside her as she listened to the boys' faint laughter and Curly's exuberant barks. "How are they managing to keep that dog out of the water while they fish?" Zen mused, sure that no fish would come anywhere near all that commotion.

Her mouth began to water as she pan-fried raw potatoes in a large skillet, then, when they were crisp, added thin wedges of tomato. She grated fresh black pepper over the pan and left it to simmer. In another skillet she cooked bacon and fried eggs over easy. She oven-toasted thick slices of Maria's homemade raisin bread. As coffee perked in the huge enamel pot, she added eggshells to clarify it, in the Swedish way. Then she went to the old chiffonier in the living room and took out one of her mother's embroidered cotton tablecloths, which had been wrapped in foil with mint leaves. She shook it outside and spread it on the oaken table that had been her grandmother's, then ran outside and gathered pussy willows, which she arranged in a vase in the center of the table. Finally she rang the old bell hanging on the porch. The loud clang echoed in the clear mountain air.

A lump formed in her throat as she watched Damon stride up the incline, a boy on either side of him, Curly gamboling behind.

"Umm, whatever that is I smell, I could eat a ton." Damon grinned, then bent down to give her a hard kiss on the mouth. When he pulled away, his expression was serious. "Don't ever leave me again."

Zen stared after him wide eyed as he released her and urged the boys upstairs to wash. Damon himself disappeared into the downstairs bathroom, emerging minutes later, before the boys were finished upstairs.

He surveyed the cabin with approval. "Nice. How did you manage to get it clean so fast?"

"The boys helped me." Zen felt all thumbs under his dark, watchful gaze. "Of course," she hurried to add, "there's much more to do. The screen on the porch is a wreck. The door is hanging off its hinges. The windows need washing." She rattled on. "I intend to—"

"I'll take care of the repairs," Damon said.

"You?" Zen's mouth dropped open. "Is Yanos coming?"

Damon looked haughtily down his nose, the bump at the bridge where he'd once smashed it playing football adding a sinister element to his good looks. "I'll do them. I'll be staying here for a while."

"The couch is too short for you," Zen said without thinking.

"We'll share the bed."

"Not a chance."

"Then you sleep on the couch," Damon replied, looking bored.

Zen stood tall and faced him squarely. "Now listen here, Damon—"

"We'll discuss it later. I'm hungry." He looked up the stairs as the two boys descended side by side. "Shall I pour the coffee?" he inquired of Zen.

"Youuu!" She whirled toward the stove, lifting the huge coffeepot with both hands.

"Put that down. I'll carry it," Damon ordered softly. He took the pot and placed it on the tripod near the open fire where it would stay warm and be within easy reach. Damon and the boys sat down while Zen brought iron skillets filled with food to the table and set them on metal trivets. Over the toast she placed a quilted warmer her mother had made.

For several moments there was silence as the four of them filled their plates and ate heartily.

"Zen, that was delicious," Damon said, rising to pour fresh coffee for her. The boys drank more milk, then decided to go out and play with Curly.

"Are your beds made?" their uncle asked. When they shook their heads, he pointed up the stairs. "Wait. Take your dishes to the sink first and scrape them."

Damon supervised them, then yawned and said that he would lie down for a while. He disappeared into the bedroom.

Zen checked on the boys, admonishing them to stay away from the water when she wasn't with them, and went back to cleaning the cabin. Today she intended to clean the storage cupboard on the back porch. It was a dirty, tedious job. By the time she was finished even her teeth felt dirty.

Before she could shower, the boys came in hungry and tired. She fed them, and then watched them go upstairs to play cards. When she checked a short time later, they were both asleep, the cards scattered between them, Curly sleeping on the braided rug between their beds.

With a sigh of relief, Zen stepped under the shower, lathering herself well. It felt so relaxing to let the warm water course over her body.

She was drying herself with a towel, when she realized she hadn't brought fresh clothing into the bathroom with her. Wrapping a bath sheet around herself, she tiptoed through the door that connected the bathroom to the bedroom, determined not to wake Damon, wincing as she imagined the remarks he would make.

It took several seconds to open the oak drawers on the old dresser where she'd stored her underthings. Mouth agape, she stared down at the neat pile of men's shirts she found there.

"I moved your things to the next drawer," Damon said from the bed. "Since you're so tiny, I didn't think you'd mind taking the three lower drawers while I take the upper three."

She turned to see him lying in bed propped up on one elbow, watching her. She moved back to her task, furious at his high-handedness. "You thought wrong," she declared. "When did you bring in your luggage? I didn't see you."

"While you were doing the dishes." His bare shoulder rose in a shrug. "I was sure you wouldn't mind."

"Well, I *do* mind." She took a step toward the bed. "This is my place, not one of the many Aristides holdings."

"I know that." He stretched slowly. Her eyes became riveted to his chest as the sheet slipped to his waist. "Comfortable bed. I didn't expect that. A little short though."

"It isn't your bed." She took another step toward him, wanting to tip him, bed and all, into the lake. "How dare you," she began, then gave an alarmed gasp and tried to leap back as Damon lunged for her.

But her timing was a tad off the mark. Damon gripped her forearm, a smile twisting his lips. He gave one short pull, and she tripped over the bath sheet and fell forward into his arms. "This is where you belong," he said softly, looking down at her, one leg draped across her middle, his hand loosening the towel from her upper body.

"The boys," Zen warned, feeling as though she was coming down with a fever.

"Are asleep," Damon stated. "I heard you tiptoe down the stairs." The triumphant heat in his eyes both angered and weakened her. "You're so beautiful . . . so mighty, but so tiny." He chuckled when she poked her tongue at him. "Eleni was twice your size, but she was a bit of fluff compared to you. You're not a Greek lady, Xenobia Driscoll Aristides."

"That's not my name," Zen croaked. "Besides, Greek women run their own households. I've seen them." She tried not to react when he inched the bath sheet from her breasts.

"Yes, but they're more subtle, more diplomatic." Damon chuckled again as his mouth nuzzled her throat. "I have the feeling that, if I displease you after we're married, you'll back my car over me."

"Yes, I will. But we're not getting married. It's just a trial engagement." Zen's temperature soared as his mouth explored her breasts.

"You have a tiny beauty spot on your left nipple...here. I've been thinking of it for three years," Damon mused, his mouth closing over the spot. "Your skin is perfect, pink and white." Damon's mouth trailed down her body, making Zen tremble with pleasure.

He pulled the bath sheet away from her, leaving her naked and vulnerable to his gaze. His bold eyes sent fire scorching through her veins. Then he pulled back his own sheet, and she saw that he was naked, too. Their bodies came together as if drawn by a force outside of their control. Zen gasped as Damon's full length pressed against her.

"Damon, the boys..." She said weakly, trying to rally her resistance.

"The door to the hall is locked."

"When did you do that?" she quizzed, hope fading fast.

"When you were showering," Damon muttered, his breathing rapid and uneven.

"Oh." As he began to kiss her instep, holding her foot like a precious jewel, Zen felt as if she were falling off the edge of the world.

"You're my wife," he murmured, suckling her toe, tickling her unbearably. He laughed deep in his throat.

"No." Zen clutched him wildly as she fell into the heady vortex Damon was creating.

"Yes, my darling..." He turned her over and caressed the backs of her knees with his mouth, making her pulse jump in response.

"I won't be controlled." Zen's voice was muffled as she writhed beneath him, her face pressed into the pillow.

"Then control me," Damon invited, sliding his hand up the back of her thigh before following with his mouth.

"That'll be the day," she replied breathlessly as she turned her face away, gasping for air.

When Damon nipped her buttocks, she squealed. "Do your worst with me, Xenobia," he challenged. "I won't fight back. I just won't let you leave me." He flipped her over again and buried his face in her abdomen. "Not ever."

"Crazy man," she whispered, taking hold of his thick hair and pulling him up to face her. "We're so different."

"We're one," he said with a growl. "I'm yours, and you'll never get rid of me."

Zen moved restlessly against the sheets. "Damon!"

"Yes, Xenobia, yes!" He caressed her parted thighs with gentle fingers, then with moist lips. Zen arched her back in astonished delight as measure upon measure of emotion twisted and burned inside her, building into white heat.

Her own hands laid claim to his body as he possessed hers. Memories of their previous lovemaking flooded back, guiding her hands as she touched him, making him groan and shudder. With growing urgency she sought to please him, her exploration of his virile form an erotic impetus to her own delight. She nibbled at his neck, then slid her mouth down his chest until she was tasting his nipples as he had tasted hers.

"Zen . . . Zen, darling . . ." Damon folded her closer, his chest heaving against her. All at once his control had broken.

He entered her, her body moist and ready for him, welcoming him, demanding him, embracing him. She held him in deep and loving incarceration; he became her slave just as she was his.

For long minutes they climbed the heavens together, gasping at the peak with pleasure that was theirs alone. The stars were laid bare before them as they gloried in sensual fulfillment.

"Damon, Damon," Zen moaned, long moments later, knowing that he had taken more than her body, that she had given more than her flesh.

"Yes, my darling wife?"

"Engaged," Zen gasped.

"Married," Damon insisted against her mouth.

Under his soothing hands her racing heart calmed, her heated skin cooled. She snuggled closer, reveling in his strength and warmth after being so very long apart.

They heard the clatter in the loft at the same time.

Zen leaped from the bed and sped across the room to the tall dresser, pulling out clothes helter-skelter, then running for the bathroom.

Damon leaned against the headboard of the bed, watching her. "Have I told you how much I love your breasts?"

"Stop it," Zen scolded, slamming the bathroom door on his laugh.

She unlocked the other door to the bathroom, which led to the hall, and called out to the boys that she was just changing her clothes and would join them in a moment. She gritted her teeth when she heard Damon chortle in the bedroom.

Before he was dressed, Zen hurried out to the boys and asked if they would like to go on a hike.

"Sure, Aunt Zeno," David agreed, delighted with the idea of putting a pack on his back with a box of graham crackers inside it.

Zen was relieved that the old canvas backpacks that had belonged to her and Eleni were still usable. She strapped a second pack on Daniel and added two cans of fruit juice.

Curly was only too glad to lead the way into the piney woods surrounding the cabin, and, although Zen was fairly certain of her direction, she marked the trees with a jackknife as her father had taught her. She explained what she was doing to the boys.

"It's very important that you guard against getting lost in an area as large as the Adirondacks," she said. "So you two must promise never to go out into the woods alone, okay?"

"Yes, Aunt Zeno," they chorused, round-eyed with excitement.

"Didn't you think I would want to come, Aunt Zeno?" Damon quizzed behind them, making Zen jump and the boys squeal. She turned to see him leaning against a maple tree.

"It's Uncle Damon," David pointed, grinning.

Daniel nodded, his smile wide.

"I–I thought you needed your sleep," Zen said stiffly, pausing at the top of a gully.

The boys followed Curly, heeding Zen's warning to stay close.

"Don't get too tired, darling," Damon whispered close behind her. "I don't want you to be worn out tonight." His chuckle sent tingles along her skin.

"Balloon-head." Zen pushed hard against his chest.

To her surprise, Damon staggered. He struggled to regain his balance, but his feet slipped on the wet mat of old leaves and pine needles, and he tumbled down the side of the gully, gathering momentum until he crashed against a tree. His leg was bent under him at a crazy angle.

Zen heard his grunt of pain even as she leaped after him. "Damon, are you all right?" she cried, aghast. She reached him in seconds, and, hearing the boys run back, she called up to them, "Stay where you are. Uncle Damon fell."

"You pushed me," he accused, regarding her with exasperated amusement. "And if you say it was an accident, I'll strangle you."

"Does anything hurt?" Zen asked anxiously as he grasped the tree trunk and rose slowly to his feet. He seemed to be favoring one foot. "You didn't break it, did you?"

"Wrenched it." Damon winced, then glanced at her with one eyebrow arched.

"You aren't faking, are you?" Zen watched him closely, suspicion and concern warring within her.

"Xenobia, that's unkind." Damon flinched and laughed as he inched back up the gully, one arm curled tightly around Zen's shoulders.

"I know you," Zen mumbled, breathing heavily as

she made the short ascent to where the boys were watching, wide-eyed.

"Will Uncle Damon have to have his dinner in bed?" Daniel asked as David ran off to get a long stick he'd seen.

"No, of course not, dear," Zen began.

"Maybe." Damon gave a woeful sigh.

"Not likely, you malingerer," Zen retorted as they began hobbling back to the cabin. "Must you put all your weight on me?" she complained, trying to mask her delight at holding him.

"I hate to be a burden." Damon's eyes glinted with deviltry as her face grew warm. "You're so cute when you blush," he cooed.

"I'm going to kick you in the other leg." Zen fumed, manipulating them past some low-hanging branches.

By the time they had covered the short distance back to the cabin, Zen was red-faced and sweaty, out of breath and out of sorts. Though he was still limping, Damon seemed in high spirits.

"Do you want to get into bed?" Zen asked as she helped him through the door and into the main room.

"No, I'll rest on the couch, maybe play crazy eights with the boys."

"Goody," Zen responded sarcastically, but her heart flip-flopped when he smiled at her.

As she chopped the vegetables for poor-man's stew, she couldn't help noticing how well Damon got along with the boys. Only a fool would fail to see the growing rapport among them, or the unfeigned affection the boys expressed for each other and for their uncle. Zen knew that she, too, shared their love. "I'll end up marrying him . . . and then that chauvinistic Greek will put me in my place," she muttered.

"Not Greek, darling, American, like you." Damon kissed her neck.

Startled, Zen lost her grip on the knife. It slipped and she cut her finger. "Look what you made me do! Are you going to call that an accident?" She swallowed hard, trying to slow her pulse.

Damon nodded and took her bleeding thumb into his mouth, sucking gently.

"Don't do that," Zen said, trying to free her hand.

"I'm fighting infection." The lazy heat in Damon's eyes sent languid warmth through her limbs.

"Indeed," Zen replied. "I have to finish cooking." She jerked away from him and sprinted for the back porch, where the barbecue utensils were stored. After filling the outdoor brick broiler with enough hardwood to cook the foil-wrapped dinner of meat, potatoes, and carrots with herbs, and spices, she lit the fire.

"Don't run away from me, darling." Damon stood behind her as she fanned the flames.

"Aaaah!" Zen jumped again. "Stop doing that. You're supposed to be resting. You can't walk."

"Yes, I can. I found a polished maple root that looks like a long shillelagh."

Zen smiled. "Daddy bought me that shillelagh at the Cooperstown Farmers Museum when I was a little girl."

"Very handy when you've sprained an ankle." Damon leaned around her to peer at the fire.

"I still think you should be resting your foot," she said.

"It's all right. I've done worse on the ski slopes."

"In Lausanne, I suppose," Zen snapped, thinking of all the beautiful women who frequented the resort.

"Gstaad, actually. We have a house there. Had you forgotten?"

"Yes." Zen turned away from him. "I'm going to slice some fruit while the fire burns down to coals."

Damon remained nearby, chatting with the boys as they played cards, then sitting on the step stool in the kitchen from where he could watch them in the main room.

By the time Zen had cut up apples, pineapples, oranges, and grapes and tossed them with a mixture of plain yogurt and honey, the fire was ready.

Dinner was a success, the fresh mountain air ensuring their good appetites.

The boys helped clean up, then joined Damon in the

living room. He fingered a book on his lap. "Would you like me to read the story of the Ancient Mariner?" he asked. "It's a poem I used to like when I was a boy."

Zen's eyes widened in surprise at his selection. How strange that they should share a special fondness for that poem. "You're my albatross," she muttered, polishing the glass in her hand and putting it in the cupboard. "If I hurt you, all bad things will happen to me. If I keep you, all bad things will happen to me." She sighed, feeling sorry for herself.

"What did you say about the albatross, Zen? Do you like Coleridge?"

"Sometimes," Zen admitted grudgingly, shaking out the towel after drying the last dish and draping it over the counter, joining Damon and the boys.

Damon began reading, and though much of the poem was lost on the boys, they seemed to enjoy it. Then he closed the book and began to explain.

"The Ancient Mariner is about a sailor who, many years ago, killed a bird that had been flying around his ship. The bird was an albatross, and after its death, the ship and the sailors on it began to have bad luck. The wind didn't fill the sails, people became ill." Damon spoke in slow, measured tones, holding the boys in thrall even as their eyes dropped with fatigue. "Many people refer to a person who has troubles as one who has an albatross around his neck. But I think the story tries to tell us to take care of the world around us—the earth, the animals, and the people."

"Like we take care of Curly?" Daniel asked yawning.

"Yes." Damon watched Zen lead the boys from the room, his face expressionless. He said good night before they climbed up the stairs, but Zen accompanied them to make sure they brushed their teeth and to listen to the prayers their grandmother had taught them to say each night.

When Zen came down from the loft, Damon was not in the living room. Assuming he was in the bathroom, she went to get fresh bedding for the couch. She was tucking in the sheets when Damon said behind her, "Forget it. We're sleeping together."

Startled, she whirled around. His dark scowl made him look like Lucifer. She drew herself up. "Now, you listen to—"

"Xenobia, please don't argue with me. Not after this afternoon."

"I'm a restless sleeper," she said, voicing the first excuse that came to mind.

"We won't be sleeping much anyway," he countered.

"Damon—"

"I am not letting you sleep without me. Even if you don't want to make love, I will not sleep without you . . . and that's the way it's going to be for the rest of our lives."

"Just like that."

"Exactly like that."

"We'll argue," she warned, taking a different tack.

"Don't underestimate us, Xenobia. We will no doubt argue every day. But that won't change anything. We'll still be in each other's arms at night."

She stared mutely up at him, unable to muster a rebuttal, her mind blank. Her sharp repartee had deserted her.

"Shall we go to bed, darling?" Damon urged softly, watching her from the bedroom doorway.

"But, your leg . . . ankle, that is. We don't want to do any damage—"

"Xenobia . . ." Damon's voice rose almost imperceptibly.

"What is it, Aunt Zeno?" David's sleepy voice drifted down the staircase.

"Nothing, dear," Zen answered, trying to keep her voice light. She glared at Damon.

"We're just going to bed, son," he called to the boy.

"'Kay. 'Night." David's voice faded.

"You said—" Zen cleared her throat. "You said that if I didn't want to . . . to make love . . . we wouldn't."

"Right." Damon leaned nonchalantly against the door frame.

"All right, then. I'm tired," Zen announced.

"So am I." Damon straightened and went into the bathroom.

Zen rummaged through an old chest of her mother's, looking for a flannel nightie. She found one packed in mint leaves and potpourri and held it up, frowning. She hated to give up the delicious sensation of sleeping naked, but she wasn't willing to risk accidentally touching Damon. One brush of his skin against hers and she would go up in flames.

She collected her soaps and the other paraphernalia she would need and when Damon opened the door, she slipped past him into the bathroom.

"Are you in such a hurry, honey lamb?" he crooned, sending shivers down her spine.

"I'm tired. Remember, I told you I was tired." Zen slammed the door on his grinning face.

She had intended to take her time preparing for bed, but when she washed her face and her body, her trembling hand slowed her even more.

When she returned to the bedroom, all was in darkness.

Taking a deep breath and fixing her eyes on the bed, she shut off the bathroom light. It was like stepping into a deep well.

She stubbed her toe against the foot of the bed. Muttering imprecations, she grabbed hold of the offended limb and hopped around on the other foot.

"For God's sake, Zen..." Damon switched on the light over the bed and scowled at her. "Now can you find your way?"

"Yes, and—"

"Then come to bed. And for God's sake, take off that horse blanket you're wearing. You'll suffocate."

"Not on your life." Zen humphed, then eased under the sheet, clinging to her side of the bed as if it were a life raft.

She closed her eyes and tried to sleep, but the nightgown twisted around her legs and pulled at her neck. She grew unbearably warm. Finally she couldn't stand it anymore. She sat up, pulled the gown over her head, and tossed it to the end of the bed.

"Even that slice of moon gives off enough light for me to see your lovely breasts, sweet," Damon murmured.

"I have a headache," Zen mumbled.

"Of course you have," Damon soothed, lying still.

Zen's head sank down on the pillow, and she stretched out, as straight and stiff as a ramrod.

"Good night, Zen."

"'Night." She swallowed dryly, her eyes wide and staring up at the darkened ceiling, where a bar of light was reflected.

She had no idea when her eyes closed. She was preoccupied with surprise and disappointment because Damon hadn't kissed her good night.

It grew colder in the wee hours of the night. Zen awoke groggy and cold in the predawn, wondering if the boys were warm. Stumbling out of bed, she pulled on a robe and went up the stairs. Curly woke up and wagged his tail, but the boys continued breathing deeply, tucked up warm in their quilted sleeping bags. Zen retraced her steps, shivering, and resolved to keep on her robe when she went back to bed.

But when she crawled under the covers, Damon's strong, warm arms came around her, unwrapping the robe from her and pulling her tight to his hard body.

"Your headache must be gone," Damon said, his lips feathering light kisses across her forehead.

"How do you know?" Zen asked, straining to keep from curving into his warmth. When he rested the flat of his hand on her buttocks, she sighed and gave in, closing her eyes in delight as his heat penetrated to her very core.

"You were cold." Damon's voice was gruff as he folded her even closer, his body sheltering hers.

"Not cold now," she mumbled. "Toasty." Her words ruffled the curling black hair on his chest.

"I'm a little more than toasty, darling," Damon crooned, rhythmically stroking her bottom.

"Living with men can be complicated," Zen observed, cuddling into his warmth.

Damon's body stiffened. "Oh? How many men have you lived with?" he asked with a casualness that failed to hide an underlying tension.

"Huh? Me?" She stretched to look up at him. His dark, brooding gaze startled her. "Purely hypothetical," she murmured and put her head back on his chest.

"Who is Seamus—that man David keeps mentioning in connection with Dublin?"

"Actually, he talks about his friend Robbie—"

"Zen, I want to know about Seamus."

"I told you, Seamus Dare is a co-worker at Deirdre's salon. He's an incredible photographer."

"I don't give a damn what he does," Damon said with a growl, his embrace tightening. "Did you live with him?"

Zen's head snapped up. "You have no right to know what I did with my life when we were apart. Have I asked you about the women you slept with while I was in Ireland?"

"Ask away." Damon's face took a grayish tinge in the pale dawn light.

"Were you celibate while I was in Ireland?"

"No," he snapped.

"My answer is the same," Zen lied without thinking, despair engulfing her. Once again his embrace tightened, crushing her. "Owww, Damon, you'll break my ribs," she cried softly.

"Damn you, Xenobia," he said gently. Then his mouth swooped down onto hers, tearing it open at once, his tongue taking ardent possession.

As his mouth trailed down her body, Zen was sure she could hear him cursing, but soon her senses were focused in another direction. A white-hot heat was coursing through her, twisting and turning, building in an intense, overwhelming crescendo.

Damon was every bit as tender as before, but this time Zen sensed a new urgency in him, a purpose, a determination that had been missing the first time. It fired them both to greater heights of passion.

Zen felt as if she were falling into a whirlpool. Part of her struggled to resist the pull. Another part of her knew it was no use. Damon held her in silken fetters. Their three years apart had not broken the bonds that united them. Three thousand miles had not separated their spirits. Something that defied time and distance and their own willful hearts held them enthralled, one to the other, for all time.

Zen reached out for him. "Damon, Damon."

"Yes...my own. I'm here. Let me love you." His mouth moved over her, sending heat through every part of her, making her gasp with pleasure, so that when he lifted his body over her, she was ready and welcoming.

All thought ceased in the onrush of sensation upon sensation that grew and grew until they tumbled together into the wild whirlpool of love, clinging to each other fiercely as shudders of release swept over them.

Zen whispered into his chest so that he couldn't hear. "Damon, I love you. I love you far, far too much to share you with anyone."

Chapter   6

AFTER THREE DAYS in Damon's company, Zen was feeling the strain. She felt as though she were walking across quicksand on stepping stones, with no firm ground anywhere. Every time she thought her feelings for him were under control, he did something to throw her off balance. Sometimes she wondered if he could read her mind, so effectively did he anticipate her moves and counteract them.

One afternoon, when the boys were napping in the loft, and Damon was resting his leg in bed, Zen decided to go down to the old dock and see if she could repair the broken slats. The day was very warm for May, so she decided to wear faded cutoff jeans and a short-sleeved cotton shirt that had been washed so many times it was almost transparent. She shrugged at her image in the mirror, aware that her breasts were barely covered, and started to pull up the zipper on her pants.

A sound stilled her hand. She turned to see Damon leaning against the doorjamb, his arms crossed on his chest. "I thought you were resting your ankle," she said.

"I was. It's rested."

"You're better, and you know it," she accused him, feeling her body tingle under his scrutiny.

"I'm returning to good health . . . under your care."

His sardonic look made her sputter. "I have things to do. I don't have time to chat."

"What are you going to do?" Damon blocked her exit from the room. "I wasn't asleep when you were creeping around gathering your clothes."

"No? Well, now you can rest." She shifted from one foot to the other in front of him. "I'm going to see if I can repair the dock."

"I'll help." He straightened from the doorjamb, looking down at her from his six-foot-plus height. "That's the sexiest set of work clothes I've ever seen." Before she could move, he hooked one arm around her and lifted her toward him to press his face to the opening of the blouse.

"I'm in a hurry," Zen protested. She swayed unsteadily when he freed her abruptly.

"You lead. I'll follow," he said.

Zen stomped past him down the hall and out the kitchen door to the enclosed back porch. She unlocked the tool cupboard and flung open the doors to reveal fairly well-stocked shelves. Some of the tools were beginning to rust but others were still shiny new.

Damon reached around her and hefted some of them. "Good ones. I'll have to clean some with oil. I think we'll be using this place a great deal once we're married. The boys like it, and so do I." He was studying the rust on a pair of pliers and didn't see Zen's stunned expression.

Damon Aristides liked a rustic cottage on a mountain lake? Remembering the pictures she'd seen of him in the gossip papers on the newsstands in Dublin, she couldn't believe it. Damon Aristides had squired beautiful women to the Riviera, to Nice, to Rome, to the Greek islands.

"Twaddle," Zen muttered, reaching for tools, nails, and a measuring tape.

"What?" Damon followed her off the porch, carrying clamps and wrenches. "What did you say?"

"Nothing." Zen flounced ahead of him down the incline, then paused. "I'd better check on the boys before I go down to the lake."

"Don't worry. I checked on them before I went to find you. Curly is up there with them, as usual." He paused, but continued to follow Zen. "You have the sweetest rear end, darling. Ummm, so nice."

"You are a crass low-life, Mr. Aristides," she retorted, angry at the secret pleasure his compliments gave her.

"Sweet buns, how you talk to your husband." Damon laughed, coming up to her side and putting his arm around her.

"Don't call me 'sweet buns'!" Zen fumed, trying to pry his arm from her middle. "And I am not your wife."

"I like it." Damon tightened his hold. "And you *are* my wife."

When they reached the narrow strip of shore near the dock, Damon released her and walked out onto the wooden structure.

"Damon, be careful. It hasn't been looked at in years," Zen called.

"I can see that." He squatted down to study the extent of disrepair. "Still, a great deal of it can be mended. It was well built."

Zen began to follow him out onto the dock, but he gestured for her to stay back. "Why can't I?" she demanded angrily.

"That temper of yours erupts at the snap of a finger, doesn't it?" He laughed at her glowering look. "Why don't you put some oil on the bolts? I'll start replacing the boards."

Zen agreed, though she was still irritated. She grimaced at the smell of the oil. "It smells like soiled kitty litter." Zen grimaced when Damon laughed at her. "Why do I put up with that man?" she muttered to herself as she coated the bolts and nuts of the supports, keeping her head averted to avoid as much of the odor as possible.

They worked on into the afternoon, Zen feeling safe and happy laboring beside Damon, delighted when she could see that the new pieces he had sawed and mitered by hand were beginning to transform the shabby pier.

"Aunt Zenooo!" David's voice called. "We want to come down with you."

"All right, dear. You and Daniel get some fruit for yourselves and a biscuit for Curly, then join us," Zen called back. She rose to her feet. She asked Damon, "Why don't I get us a cold drink? Are you thirsty?"

"I'd love some of that well water."

"Not Dom Perignon?"

"That's for later, love, when I'm peeling your clothes from your lovely body, a piece at a—"

"Stop it." Zen threw down the capped oil can and wiped her hands on her cutoffs. "I'll bring you a beer."

"That or the well water." Damon went back to sawing. He'd taken his shirt off, and his back glistened bronze in the sun.

Zen paused, watching the smooth motion of his shoulder and arm as he pushed and pulled the saw in rhythmic strokes. "I suppose you never get sunburned."

"Never. I have tough skin," Damon replied, cocking an amused eyebrow at her.

"Do you like to sunbathe?"

"Sometimes. But only after I've worked out in the water, or on it . . . and I never wear a suit, love."

"You must be arrested regularly."

"Darling, many of the beaches around the world allow nude sunbathing."

"Trust you to find them," Zen snapped, turning away when he chuckled.

"Yes, I think I have been to most of them."

"Viper," she whispered. She forced a smile to her face when she reached the boys, who were cavorting down the incline.

"We brung you an apple, Aunt Zeno. One for Uncle Damon, too."

"Thank you, Daniel, but say, 'We brought you an

apple,' not 'brung.' Take them down to the lake, and I'll bring some fruit juice and crackers."

David thought it over. "And cheese. And maybe another biscuit for Curly, and—"

"I'll try to bring everything," Zen interrupted, hoping to cut short his lengthening list.

Zen washed her hands and face. Then, loaded down with the food David had requested, she returned to the lakeshore.

The boys were sitting on the end of the dock talking to Damon, and tossing a stick to Curly, who never seemed to tire of leaping into the cold water and retrieving it.

Damon took the cold beer she handed him and held the icy can to his forehead. "Any moment now I may join Curly in the water."

"Don't be foolish. You'd freeze," Zen admonished.

"Will we come up here later, when the water is warm, Uncle Damon?" David asked.

"Sure. We'll come up on weekends. We'll get a boat, too."

Zen opened her mouth to say that she wasn't sure she would be doing that, but one look at the joyful expression on the boys' faces stilled her retort.

Zen spread a cloth on the deck and unpacked the things she had brought.

"I like it here," Daniel said. "I like being with you, Aunt Zeno."

Zen blinked back a sudden moistness in her eyes. "And I like being with you, too, love."

Damon leaned down into the water and washed his hands, then joined them. He startled Zen by lying down with his head in her lap. "Yes, I like it here. We'll come often," he agreed softly.

The days continued to grow warmer, but the evenings were often chilly.

Each night Zen slept in Damon's arms. She had stopped protesting when he reached for her in the dark, but each time they made love, she felt a sense of defeat. She would have to give him up someday. She would never be able to hold him. But it would be so hard, now that she had belonged to him so completely. For him the feeling would pass. He would go on to someone else. But for her there would be no one else—just Damon.

He seemed in no hurry to end their holiday, although Zen knew he had important responsibilities as director of the Aristides businesses.

One morning when the boys had gone out to play after eating breakfast, Zen approached Damon on the front porch, where he was repairing some screens. "I think we should go back now," she said.

"Do you, darling?" He put down the tack hammer and hooked his arm around her waist. "All right, we'll go home. I've missed two important meetings that I remember . . . But we'll be coming back here. The boys thrive on the mountain air. I feel good myself. How do you feel? With that honey glow to your skin, why should I ask, right?"

"Right," she agreed out loud. But in her mind she shouted, I feel as if I've been emotionally drawn and quartered.

The boys didn't make a fuss about leaving, since their uncle assured them they would be coming back to the cottage during the summer.

The day before they were to leave, the weather turned cold, and work on the dock, although almost finished, stopped.

Damon bundled the boys up in winter coats and boots, and took them for a walk, Curly at their side. Zen stayed in the cabin and made chicken soup from scratch. She chopped every vegetable available, except the fresh cooked beets, which she intended to slice and marinate in oil and vinegar with onions and chives.

While the stock and vegetables were simmering, she packed some of the boys' things, to save time in the morning.

She was back in the kitchen stirring the soup, then lifting a wooden spoon to taste it, when Damon crooned in her ear, "Feed me." Startled, Zen jerked her hand and spilled some of the soup.

"Damon! We both could have been burned." She

frowned at him as she lifted the spoon to his mouth.
"Where are the boys?"

"Mmmm, good. Ahh...hot! The boys are lying in
front of the fire with Curly." Damon sipped the rest of
the soup off the spoon, then kissed her, his mouth opening on hers. "Thank you...for the soup."

"Yes." Zen swung around to gaze down at the bub-
bling kettle, not seeing the vegetables floating there.
Damon's face filled her mind.

That evening, Zen served dinner from a blanket spread
out in front of the fire. Damon and the twins helped bring
out the food, but with a great deal of teasing and giggling.

"Curly can eat with us," David decided. Daniel nodded.

"Curly will eat outside," Damon corrected. "Then,
when we've cleaned up our dishes and taken our walk,
Curly can join us by the fire."

David frowned at his uncle, but, seeming to decide
that arguing wouldn't change Damon's mind, he nodded.

The soup and hard rolls disappeared like magic, and,
to Zen's surprise, so did the beet salad. For dessert there
were apples, grapes, and cheese, which they ate after
Damon and the boys had cleared away and washed most
of the dishes, as Zen watched from the doorway.

"Stop looking so surprised, Zen," Damon chided her.
"I know how to wash dishes. I lived in Alaska for a time,
up near Barrow. I learned how to cook and take care of
myself. I also backpacked to Alice Springs in Australia
with a friend. Dug for opals, studied the aborigines..."
He shrugged.

"I never knew that." Zen took a chair in the kitchen
and watched the boys dry the plates.

"Was it scary?" Daniel asked.

Damon shook his head. "Australia is awesome, not
scary. I loved it...and I'm going to take Aunt Zeno
there on a trip someday."

Zen felt her neck redden as Damon chuckled and both
boys cried, "Take me, too."

After they went for a walk, the boys stretched out in

front of the fireplace, and Damon held up a guitar he'd found in a cupboard. He raised his eyebrows at Zen.

"My father's," she explained, reaching for it. She twisted the string screws to see if it could be tuned after such a long time and after having experienced such extremes of temperature in the cabin. Several minutes passed before she decided it might be playable. She strummed a few chords and found it in fairly good tune. When she sang the mountain song "Shenandoah," the poignant words and melody carried her away. She was taken aback when Damon's rich baritone joined her lilting soprano.

It took all her courage to continue playing. His voice seemed to reach out to her and pull her into himself, as though now her blood ran with his.

The boys applauded and sang a song Daniel had learned in school and taught to David.

When the boys could no longer keep their eyes open, Damon carried them up stairs, Curly at his heels, Zen following behind them.

In no time the twins were asleep, the dog curled up on the floor between the beds.

"Let's have some wine." Damon went out to his car and returned with a bottle of French champagne. "A friend of mine, Marcel Daubert, has vineyards in Provence," he explained. "This is his family's wine."

"Did you meet him when you were at Oxford?"

Damon paused in opening the bottle. "How did you know I went there?"

"Eleni told me you were a Rhodes scholar." Zen was tickled that Damon seemed discomfited. "She said you were the brainy one of the family," Zen added, deliberately provoking him.

"And no doubt she told you I don't like to talk about it," Damon said dryly, watching her.

"She might have." Zen smiled. "But why wouldn't you want to talk about something as prestigious as being a Rhodes scholar?"

"My mother and grandmother and uncles all talked of nothing else whenever they were in my company. Finally

I convinced my mother to spread the word that I didn't want to talk about it anymore."

"Poor baby," Zen soothed.

"Little demon." Damon reached and grabbed her before she could get away. He sat down with her in his lap, holding her with one arm while his other hand touched the pleasure points of her body. "Tease me, will you?"

Zen laughed, then gasped. "Stop it, Damon. The boys..."

He glanced up the stairs, then back at her. "All right. For the moment." He reached behind him and hefted the guitar. "Play a song for me."

Zen played and sang, and Damon sang with her. For a short time the real world seemed to fade away, and they escaped to another realm that contained them alone.

When at last they prepared for bed, Damon's arm curled around her waist; hers rested across his broad back. The champagne was gone, and the evening had taken on a luster that had nothing to do with wine.

"You may have dark circles under your eyes in the morning," Damon said as he began to undress her, keeping her standing in front of him. "No, don't cover your breasts...please." He leaned down to take her nipple into his mouth.

His touch made her body tremble. She closed her eyes as he released her breast and knelt in front of her to slide her jeans, then the bikini panties, down her legs.

"Naked or dressed, *agape mou,*" Damon said in guttural Greek. "You are Venus to me." He pressed a kiss to her abdomen, then stood and flung off his own clothes and caught her to him again, leading her to the bed and sinking with her down into its comfort.

The night was long and beautiful. Zen could deny him nothing. But each time their bodies separated, she felt an overwhelming sense of loss that filled her with despair.

The next morning was sunny, crisp, and cold. The lake sparkled like a sapphire.

Zen packed quickly and easily. Though she tried, she couldn't smother the sadness that engulfed her at the thought of leaving. These days with Damon and the boys had been some of the happiest she had ever known. She might return to the cottage with David and Daniel, but surely she would never return with Damon.

"Now remember, Zen, I'll be right behind you," he said, pointing to the map. "This is the first leg of the trip. We'll stop there." He punched a point with his index finger.

She nodded, then looked up at him, trying to keep her face expressionless. "Fine. We'll see you at the restaurant near Johnsburg."

He smiled down at her, studying her intently. "You'll never be free of me, Xenobia. You're tied to me." He turned to call the boys and the dog, then checked once more to ensure that the doors and windows were locked and the pump shut off.

Zen stood frozen to the spot, watching him, wanting both to strike him and to cling to him. She hated their hot–cold relationship, the ambivalence that kept her emotions seesawing from high to low.

When both boys and the dog were settled in the Cherokee, she began to climb into the car. Then she felt herself being lifted into the seat.

"Are you sure this isn't too tough for you to maneuver? Wouldn't you rather drive the Ferrari?"

God, no, she thought, shaking her head. She needed the distraction of the boys—their laughter, bickering, and interminable questions.

Reluctantly Damon let her go and climbed into his own car.

The drive to the secondary road was uneventful, but, though the highway wasn't as busy as it would be on the weekends, there were still enough cars to demand Zen's full attention.

When they arrived at Harley's Garage, she turned in to fill up on gas.

"Hi, there. Nice to see you folks again." Harley

squinted up the road as the Ferrari pulled in after them. "I see your husband found you all right."

"Ah, yes." Zen smiled weakly, letting the boys out of the car and snapping a leash on Curly.

"What's that for?" Damon asked, nodding toward the dog scooper and taking the lead from her.

"I use it to clean up after Curly when we're traveling," Zen explained. She stifled a giggle as Damon grimaced, shook his head, and walked away. The thought of the great Damon Aristides cleaning up after a dog threatened to send her into peals of laughter.

Damon glared back at her. "There's always tonight, Xenobia, when we're in bed," he warned.

"We'll be at your mother's house, in our own rooms," she retorted.

He shook his head. "The house is mine, and you *will* be sleeping with me—either in my suite or yours."

Zen made a face at his back. "Go suck an egg," she muttered, then sprinted for the bathroom where the boys were, sensing that Damon had heard her.

The boys had decided that they didn't want to be encumbered by their seat belts, and they were arguing the point with Zen when Damon returned with Curly.

"Don't let me hear you talk that way again," he said more sternly than he had ever spoken to them. "When it comes to safety, there is no arguing. Understood?"

"Yes, Uncle Damon," the boys murmured, chastened.

During the rest of the trip, they stopped at intervals to stretch their legs and feed the boys. Still, David and Daniel became cranky and rambunctious as the trip lengthened. They took only a short nap. Then they began arguing. Several miles farther on, Damon passed Zen and signaled for her to pull over.

"I'm taking over the Cherokee, Zen. You drive the Ferrari."

She gulped. "I've never driven such a sophisticated machine."

"Don't worry. You know how to operate a standard shift, so I'll just adjust the seat for you, explain a few of the features, and you'll be on your way. We have only about a hundred miles to go, and I can see that the boys are beginning to act up."

Zen listened to his instructions with half an ear, feeling more inclined to watch his bent head and the way the sun glistened on his hair.

At last she was alone in the car, watching Damon signal and pull onto the highway. She did the same, keeping a safe distance behind the Cherokee.

When they had traveled several miles, a Camaro passed her carrying two young men who whistled and called out to her. Zen ignored them, but they pulled in between her and the Cherokee and began making gestures out the window, signaling for her to pull over. When she had the chance, she pulled out in front of them and floored the Ferrari, letting it leap ahead. The Camaro began to speed up.

Zen glanced at Damon as she pulled up alongside the Cherokee. He, too, motioned for her to pull over to the side of the road.

When she pulled to a stop, the Camaro pulled over as well. Apparently the young men didn't notice that Damon had stopped, too.

Even as he was stepping from the Cherokee, a State Trooper arrived. Zen wondered if Damon had called him on the CB. The men in the Camaro made as though to return to their car, but Damon collared them and told the officer that the men had tried to intimidate his wife.

"Hey, Mac, we didn't know she was yours," said one of the young men.

"You sure knew she wasn't yours . . . and that it's against the law to play games like that on the highway," Damon retorted angrily, the words coming from his mouth like bullets, his hands clenching and unclenching at his sides. "Officer, I'd like to charge these men with harassment."

Both men shifted restlessly on their feet, their faces flushed with anger.

The policeman wrote busily on his pad. Damon assured him that his lawyer would visit the State Police headquarters to see that the men were charged as he felt they should be.

Zen wasn't sure, but she thought she saw the trooper's lips twitch as he read the men their rights. Was he enjoying this?

When they finally turned into the long circular drive leading to the Aristides estate, Zen could see Sophie standing in the drive, her hands clasped in front of her. Thag was there, too, as usual, but this time he seemed filled with anticipation as he shifted restlessly from one foot to the other. Zen was glad he'd stayed. She hoped to get to know him better. Yanos was leaning on his rake, and Maria and Lona stood farther up the steps.

The Ferrari and the Cherokee pulled to a stop, and the twins tumbled out.

"We had fun!" David exclaimed as he hugged his grandmother.

Daniel hugged her, too. "David and me slept in the loft. Aunt Zeno and Uncle Damon slept downstairs."

Zen's cheeks burned with embarrassment as Sophie's eyes turned to hers, one eyebrow arching just the way Damon's did. Pythagoras was grinning.

Curly jumped down from the van and immediately watered the rose bed.

"Damn you," Damon said mildly, looking amused. "If you kill those roses, Yanos will have your ears." His eyes caught Zen's, where she was still standing beside the Ferrari. "Come over here, darling, and tell Mother what a good time we had."

"We did, we did," Daniel answered for her. "And Uncle Damon says we can go back when the weather is warmer." He looked around him. "It's warmer here, isn't it?"

"That's because you were in the mountains where the air is cool," Thag told him.

"Curly likes the lake, too, Nonna. Can you come with us next time?" David asked as his grandmother turned to lead both boys into the house.

"Yes, indeed, that would be very nice," she replied.

David paused on the top step, frowning. "You'll have to sleep with Aunt Zeno and Uncle Damon. They have the biggest bed."

"David," Zen said, "it's time to get washed for dinner." She wanted to die from embarrassment.

"I'm hungry," he announced plaintively.

"Come along with me," Lona offered. "I have nice shiny apples up in your room with wedges of cheese."

"Oh, goody." Daniel smiled at his old nurse, trying to smother a yawn.

"Come on, darling. We'll take a shower before we have a cocktail," Damon said, placing a strong arm around Zen's shoulders. He guided her into the foyer and up the stairs.

"Stop it," she stage-whispered, trying to dig in her heels. "I haven't even spoken to your mother or—"

"That's all right, Xenobia. We'll talk when you come down again," Sophie called.

Zen tried to look over her shoulder at the older woman, but Damon was taking her up the steps so fast she caught only a fleeting glance of the enigmatic face. "This is very embarrassing. Did you hear what David said?" Zen whispered as they went down the corridor leading them to their room. "I am not staying in your apartment, Damon. Surely you can see—"

"Then I'll stay in yours. Even though the bed may be too short."

"Don't be ridiculous. The bed is monstrous . . . What? You are *not* staying in my room!"

"We're sleeping together."

"No!" She shook her head until she thought her neck would snap. "I can't do it. I'll move out first."

Damon's expression grew as dark as midnight. "Why is it so bad to sleep with me now when we slept together at the cottage?"

"Your mother wasn't at the cottage, Damon. And don't look at me like that. I won't change my mind. So, which shall it be? Do I get a hotel room or do I sleep alone?"

His mouth tightened with anger and frustration. "I

don't like being pushed around, Zen. That's the one thing I will not tolerate." He spun on his heel and strode down the hall that led to double doors and beyond to his quarters.

"I don't like it either. You remember that," Zen called after him, watching his broad shoulders stiffen as he paused. He pushed open the double doors with a crash that made her flinch.

Zen stumbled into the shower, letting the steamy water pour down on her, feeling bruised in every muscle.

When she emerged a long time later, she felt a little more relaxed and in control.

Maria had already put most of her things away. "I thought you would want me to press this dress, Kyria." She gestured at the shoes and underthings she'd laid out on the bed.

"Isn't that a little too formal for dinner with the family?" Zen pointed to the grape-colored silk dress Maria was holding.

"There are guests this evening, Kyria." Maria left before Zen could question her further.

Yawning, she shrugged and flopped face down on the bed. Her body felt as flaccid as well-done spaghetti.

Damon's face appeared in her mind as she closed her eyes. Every pore, every laugh line, was familiar to her.

The phantom Damon laughed with her; then his face turned to sculpted stone. His eyes lost their gleam.

"You've run away from me once too often, Xenobia," he said. "Now I don't want you."

"You can't go away," Zen pleaded with him in her dream. "You're my albatross. I left you three years ago and, deep inside, I've been unhappy ever since. If you leave me again, I won't be able to bear it. Come back, Damon." Zen called to him and called to him. "I don't mean you're my good luck. You're my bad," she wailed in her dream. She saw the majestic albatross and whimpered in her sleep.

Suddenly, she sat up in bed, aware that the dream was true. If Damon left her, life would have no meaning.

She shook herself fully awake and straightened the covers on the bed, then reached for a robe to wear while she put on her makeup. Her eye caught the grape-colored dress hanging on the clothes tree, its silky flounces moving at the least breath of air.

The dress was street length but designed for evening wear. The off-the-shoulder ruffle was repeated in a diagonal sweep around her body from one shoulder to the hem. Zen slipped the dress over her head. It clung to her form like a gentle caress. With it she wore the pink sapphire earrings which had belonged to her sister and which Damon had given to her. She twisted her hair into a coil at the back of her head.

Taking a deep breath, she stepped into the hallway. Would she have time to visit the boys? She saw Lona coming from their room. "Are they sleeping?" she asked.

"Yes. I fed them some soup after they ate their apples and cheese. They are so tired . . . but it's a good kind of tired. I have never seen Daniel look so bright and healthy. They need each other, don't they, miss?"

"Yes, they do," Zen replied softly, a wrenching sadness welling up inside her. It was true. The boys did need each other. They needed to grow together, to go to school, to play, to discover each other. The words echoed in her head as she descended the stairs.

Blindly, her thoughts like smoke clouding her mind, Zen pushed open the double doors of the living room and was assailed by voices and strange faces. Surprised, she hesitated on the threshold. Where had all these people come from?

"There you are, darling," Damon said, stepping toward her and pulling her close to his side in a powerful embrace.

"Who are these people?" Zen asked through suddenly dry lips.

"Our guests. They've come to help us celebrate."

"That's nice." Zen glanced around her and realized that she recognized only about three people in the room. She turned back to Damon. "Celebrate what?"

"Our forthcoming marriage. Darling, I want you to meet a colleague of mine. Vince, this is Xenobia Driscoll, my fiancée. Zen, my love, this is Vince Dante, my partner in the Olympus Fishery."

"Fish?" Zen repeated stupidly, her head whirling. The room and the smiling faces in it seemed to be distorted, as if seen through a fun house mirror. She swayed and felt Damon's arm tighten around her.

"Yes. And this is Terry Riedle, vice-president of Venus Airlines."

"Planes?" Zen felt as though she had no control over her facial muscles. Her smile seemed to be slipping sideways, her eyes were heavy, and her lips felt like plastic.

"Must you keep repeating what I say?" Damon whispered in her ear.

"What?" Zen looked up at him, trying to focus. When someone held out a drink, she took it without thinking and tipped the iced liquid down her throat. She started to choke, and Damon patted her back and took the empty glass from her hand.

"I never knew you were a drinker," he commented, when she took another glass from a passing tray. "No one should toss off martinis on the rocks as though they were water."

"I don't expect you to believe me, but I thought it *was* water until I'd already taken a swallow." Zen lifted the full glass to her mouth, but paused when she saw the twist of lemon floating in it. She shrugged and sipped the bitter brew of gin and vermouth.

"Why would I not believe you, love?" Damon leaned over and took her lips, his tongue invading her mouth at once.

"Come, come, Damon...Xenobia. Not now," Pythagoras admonished gently. "Sophie is about to make the announcement." He smiled at Zen when she swayed in Damon's arms.

"Right. We're coming." He urged her into the center of the throng, where Sophie stood instructing everyone to take a glass of champagne.

"I am delighted to invite you all to my son's wedding, which will take place in two weeks," she announced.

Zen glared at them all. "Not a chance," she murmured. But her voice failed to carry over the chorus of congratulations and best wishes.

Chapter 7

"AND WHEN IS the shower? I suppose you'll expect me to have it," Damon's Aunt Dalia said sourly to Zen. She turned to Sophie. "She doesn't even look Greek."

Zen swallowed more of her martini, squinted to get her bearings on Aunt Dalia's position and started for the woman, fists clenched. "You know what you can do with—" Zen was jerked back into familiar arms and pressed against a hard chest, her words smothered in a silk dinner jacket.

"What did she say?" Aunt Dalia lifted her classic chin and looked down her patrician nose.

"She said there isn't much time if we're to have the shower before the wedding, and if you feel it's too much . . ." Damon held tightly to Zen, lovingly pressing his finger over her lips.

"Me? Not be able to hold the traditional couple's party for the bride and groom? Ridiculous! We'll have it on next Tuesday. My secretary will call everyone." Aunt Dalia gave a satisfied sniff. "Is Friday the day you're to be married?"

"Yes. In the evening by a judge who's a friend of mine. Here at the house," Damon told her.

"Of course you will have a religious ceremony at some later date." Aunt Dalia gazed at them with disapproval.

Zen freed her mouth. "You can go—"

Damon bent to kiss her, wincing only slightly when Zen bit his lip. He lifted his head and smiled at his aunt. "She said it's getting stuffy in here. Perhaps we'd better get some air."

"Your lip is bleeding." Aunt Dalia looked askance at her nephew. "In my day we saved such things for the bedroom."

"Xenobia is very earthy," Damon observed, only blinking when Zen kicked him in the shin.

"Loose. That's what the world is today, loose." Aunt Dalia humphed and turned away to speak to her nephew Sandor, who was proffering a drink to his aunt and ogling Zen at the same time.

Zen had never liked the oily Sandor, but now she beamed at him and beckoned him to her side.

Sandor waved his lighter close to Aunt Dalia's hair, nearly setting her on fire, then hurried over to Zen and Damon. "If you have guests to speak to, Damon, I will keep Zen company."

"No," Damon barked.

"Lovely idea," Zen said at the same time, moving forward as much as Damon's arm would allow. "Let me go, Damon dear. I would like to talk to your cousin."

"Sandor," Damon said casually, releasing her, his teeth coming together with a snap, "if you keep looking at Xenobia that way, I will blacken both your eyes . . . here . . . now . . . in this room."

Sandor looked at his tall, well-built cousin and would have moved away, but Zen clutched his arm just as another guest demanded Damon's attention and pulled him aside.

Zen needed to clutch something. The unaccustomed gin made her feel as though she were crossing the deck of a ship at sea.

"You have lovely breasts, Xenobia," Sandor murmured boldly in her ear.

Zen's eyes widened in shock at his audacity. "Are you adopted, Sandor?" she asked casually. "No one in this family talks in such a fashion. And incidentally, if Damon hears you speak that way, he's liable to beat your brains in."

She whirled away from Sandor—right into Sophie. "Oh! Excuse me. Ah...about that announcement."

"I know you said you would play the piano for us after dinner," Sophie gushed, "but so many of the family are dying to hear you play now."

Sophie urged her toward the mammoth Steinway. "Eleni played, not me," Zen whispered. "I play the guitar...and not very well."

Sophie ignored her and clapped her hands for attention. "Xenobia has consented to play for us," she announced loudly.

"She doesn't play very well, as I remember," Aunt Dalia warned the assembled guests, earning a glare from Zen.

"I'll play...and Zen will sing," Damon said unexpectedly. "Come, darling. Would you like to sit next to me or stand at the side of the piano?"

"I'd like to get a bus to Cleveland," Zen muttered.

"Why is she talking to herself, Sandor?" Aunt Dalia trumpeted. "She was never too bright as a child, as I recall."

Damon seemed amused by the dark look Zen shot his aunt. "Your family is the most irritating group of cretins," she mumbled between clenched teeth.

"Ignore her," Damon said. "I do. Now tell me, is there anything in this mountain of sheet music you would like me to play?"

Zen was about to tell him she didn't care what he played when her eye caught the title *Songs of Ireland* on a thick book. She took it from the stack and began leafing through it. She pointed to a song and swallowed to moisten her throat.

"Are you sure you wouldn't like to sing something Greek?" Damon laughed when she curled her lip.

"I'll leave that to you," she said, then listened to the introduction, remembering the night when Seamus and several other Irish friends of hers had gathered at her apartment and sung around the piano for much of the evening, even allowing David to sing with them. The words of the ballad had remained in her memory, and her untrained but pure soprano filled the room with the poignant melody.

Zen was so lost in the words that at first she didn't notice when Damon's baritone joined her. The sweet tune came as natural as breathing as he sang the words to "The Isle of Innisfree."

They sang other songs from the book, and Zen felt such a pull between them that she forgot for a moment that she was angry with Damon and his family. She even forgot that there were other people in the room.

When she signaled to Damon that she could sing no more, he rose from the piano and turned her to face the applause.

Sophie came forward to take her hands. "And did you learn those lovely songs from your friends in Dublin?" she asked.

"Yes." Zen smiled in remembrance. "Seamus Dare and some others used to gather at least once a week, and we would sing the old songs, some in Irish. David knows a few Irish songs."

"You saw Seamus Dare once a week?" Damon asked, his voice like velvet-covered steel.

"More frequently than that." Zen laughed. "I worked with him. He would often come home with me to visit David. They were great friends."

"Were they?" Damon's angry words made Zen and Sophie regard him in surprise.

Zen opened her mouth to speak, but Sophie interrupted. "Dinner, everyone." She cleared her throat. "It's time for dinner." She hooked her arm through Zen's and pulled her away, calling to Damon over her shoulder,

"My son, you will kindly escort your Aunt Dalia and your Aunt Sophronia. Zen will sit between Vincent and Terence."

"You needn't lead me away from him," Zen protested. "I know his damn temper is firing up again. I don't know why, and I don't give a damn. Your son is the most capricious, volatile, unstable . . ." Zen accompanied Sophie to the dining room, still listing Damon's many faults.

"He's jealous," his mother said.

"Bull chips!" Zen expostulated, then clapped her hand over her mouth in chagrin.

In all her years, she had never dreamed of using that particular expression. "You use such colorful language, Xenobia," Sophie said calmly, taking her place at the head of the table.

Zen felt her face burn with embarrassment. "Forgive me. I didn't mean—"

"Tut, tut, child, I meant no censure." Sophie caught and held Zen's gaze. "I'm glad you're with us, Xenobia. You have brought life and laughter to this house. Even my friend Pythagoras says he can't remember when Daniel ever laughed as he has laughed since David arrived. It is good." Sophie patted Zen's hand on the snowy damask tablecloth, then gestured to the maid to begin serving.

They had moussaka and a rack of lamb with rosemary and lemon, but most of the other dishes were either American or Continental. As was the custom in the Aristides home, there were several courses consisting of fish, vegetables, and fruit as well as meat.

Zen fully appreciated the food after having cooked for herself at the cabin. She complimented both Maria and Sophie.

"Soon you will be directing us, Kyria Xenobia," Maria said with the ease of a life-long retainer. She had helped to raise both Damon and Davos.

Zen coughed and reached for her water glass. She shook her head.

"Of course you will, Xenobia." Sophie patted her back

and gestured to Yanos, who was acting as butler for the evening, to refill her wine and water glasses. "It is time I retired from running this house and traveled. I want to turn it over to you, just as I turned my business interests over to my son."

There were choruses of "Good idea" and "Just the thing to do" from various guests.

"I don't think you should retire," Zen protested, her eyes watering from her coughing. "Do you, Damon?"

"I think it would be good for Mother to travel," he said. "She will still have her apartment in the house and can come back any time to visit us and the boys."

"I think it is a good idea," Pythagoras agreed. He looked startled when Zen glared at him.

Tiny Aunt Sophronia, who was said to have Albanian blood, leaned forward in her chair and fixed Zen with her eyes. "It is well past time that you tended to your duties, young woman."

"Well, of all the—"

"Darling, you're going to love the dessert," Damon interrupted, rising from his chair to come around in back of hers. "In fact, I want you to be surprised, so I'm going to cover your eyes."

"Youuu, you're covering ma mouf . . ." Zen glowered up at him, pulling at his hands.

"Ah, here's Maria. Just in time," Damon announced.

Zen freed her mouth at last and took a deep breath to tell Damon what she thought of him and his family, but he reached for the tray Maria was carrying and pushed a honey cake into her mouth. "There! I knew you'd love it." He looked up at Maria. "She loves them."

Zen was aware that all eyes were on her as she pulled the sticky cake out of her mouth. She licked the honey from her lips, camouflaging her awkwardness behind a napkin.

"What's she doing now, Sandor?" Aunt Dalia bellowed. "She's a strange creature. Don't know what Damon sees in her."

"I do." Sandor smacked his lips. Damon's onyx eyes

bore down on him like twin mortars on a target. Sandor laughed nervously. Damon ground his teeth.

"Damon, do take your seat," his mother said, frowning.

"Mother, I think it would be nice if we all had coffee and liqueur in the living room," he suggested.

Maria brought Zen a finger bowl while Yanos distributed them to the other guests. "Let me help you, Kyria Xenobia," Maria said.

"Ah . . . thank you. I can manage." Zen glanced over her shoulder at Damon. "I intend to have a mail bomb put into the In-box in your office," she said in dulcet tones.

"Darling, how sweet! Of course you can buy me a betrothal gift. I think that's very nice."

Zen rose with the others to leave the dining room. Damon kept hold of her elbow. "Release me, you savage," she demanded.

"Love, I thought you liked it when I touched you," Damon baited her.

"Stop that!" Zen caught the narrow-eyed glances of Damon's two aunts. "Your family despises me."

He was unperturbed. "I don't give a damn what they think."

"They own stock in Olympus Limited," Zen said, holding back as they approached the living room.

"If you're worried that I can't support you and the boys, my love, forget it." Damon's thick eyebrows came together over his nose; white lines bracketed his mouth.

"Don't be an ass," she retorted. "I just don't see why you want to be tied to someone who will be stared at by the family at every get-together." She fell silent.

Damon shrugged. "If they annoy you, we'll avoid my family. Of course, I'll have to arrange to see my mother with the boys now and then."

"Damon." Zen's throat tightened. "I . . . I would never try to separate the boys from your mother. I'm not like that."

He halted in front of the double doors to the living room, in full view of the occupants, who were turning slowly to observe them. "I know you hold the best interests of both boys as your primary concern. I never thought otherwise of you." He kissed her full on the mouth, his tongue chasing hers lazily.

Zen felt as though someone had set fire to her inside. Her blood seemed to be burning up.

"Was Damon always so . . . so loose, Sophie?" Aunt Dalia asked disdainfully.

"Do you not remember how it was when we were in love, Sister?" Sophie asked, raising her chin.

"Yes . . . yes, but we were not wantons like that . . . that one."

Zen pulled free of Damon. "Now, see here Aunt Dalia." She stalked into the room and stopped directly in front of the stalwart Greek woman. "You've been criticizing Damon and me all night, and I've been very patient." She turned to glare at Damon when he laughed. "But I've had enough."

"I, also, have had enough, Sister," Sophie interrupted. "I want you to come to my son's wedding and give the couple's party, but if you don't want to, someone else can."

Silence, thick, heavy silence, filled the room.

"I will give the couple's party, as I always do." Dalia sat down on the settee.

Sophie gave one curt nod and sat down next to her. "Xenobia will pour the tea," she announced.

"Good Lord," Damon whispered, backing away as if Zen's pouring tea would place him in danger.

Zen spilled some tea in the saucers. Dalia and Sophronia rolled their eyes. The other cousins drew closer and began to chat with Zen. She had no real trouble until she handed Damon his tea. Had she not looked up at him and seen the black heat in his eyes, she might have muddled through, she told herself, but she did look at him. The cup wobbled on the saucer, and she spilled hot tea on his wrist.

"Aaaagh! Damn it, Zen. I knew I shouldn't have taken tea."

"You should have asked for coffee," Aunt Dalia agreed

brusquely, her lips pursed as she presided over the silver coffeepot. "Greeks should drink coffee."

"Thank you." Damon grimaced at his aunt, then frowned down at Zen. "Stop mopping at me."

"You need some lotion." When he tried to pull his arm free, Zen thrust out her jaw. She saw Sandor place his scotch on the table and spied the ice cubes in his drink. "Pardon me, I need that." She reached into the glass and drew out an ice cube. After wrapping it in a napkin, she pressed it on Damon's skin. Part of her was appalled that she could do such a crass thing, but concern for Damon was uppermost in her thoughts.

"Damn it all, I just poured that drink," Sandor complained.

Zen ignored him. She lifted Damon's hand to her mouth and kissed the red spot.

He gasped and leaned over her. "Do that again, please."

"Sophie, I cannot stay in this house if they are going to continue to make love in public," Dalia said in stentorian tones.

"They are like this all the time," Sophie answered serenely.

"You must not be offensive, Xenobia." Aunt Sophronia sniffed. "Ours is a proud family."

"Goat chips, Sophronia," Pythagoras drawled, smiling at Zen and receiving a smile from her in return. "If you intend to stay in this house at any time in the future, you will have to become accustomed to seeing displays of affection. We thrive on it here." He moved closer to Sophie.

"My dear departed brother Dmitri, who was your husband, Sophie, would not approve of such looseness." Sophronia's pursed mouth looked like a prune.

To Zen's surprise, Sophie bit her lips and stepped away from Thag, looking distressed.

"Sophronia Aristides, if you think to upset Sophie, cease," said Pythagoras. "We will be married soon, and I will take it ill if anyone upsets my future wife." He gave each guest a warning look.

"I didn't know they were getting married," Zen whispered to Damon.

"It's about time he forced mother off the fence." Damon smiled down at her. "That's the only way to handle a woman—throw her over your shoulder and cart her away."

Zen raised her chin, prepared to do battle with him, but she paused when she caught him grinning at her. She took a deep breath. "If you're trying to bait me, it won't work."

"It usually does. Let's go to bed."

Zen gasped and glanced nervously around the room, but most of the family was staring at Sophie, whose face had turned brick red. "Not in your mother's house," Zen whispered.

"How many times must I tell you that this is my home, under my name, and in two weeks it will be your home as well."

"What do you mean?" Zen's head snapped back to him.

"It means I've instructed my lawyers to place this home and the apartment in London, plus a twenty percent share in my holdings, in your name on our wedding day."

"No." Zen shook her head, aghast. "I don't want anything. I can earn my own way. I won't be paid—"

"Stop babbling, darling. I know all about your independence, and your lack of interest in material things, but I fully intend to protect you. If anything happened to me, my enemies would try to cut you out of everything. You would win in the end, because my will is solid, but in the meantime a long litigation would be very distressing. This way no matter what happens there will be no discomfort. You will have your own property and money, deeded to you in my lifetime."

"Don't talk this way." Zen wrung her hands, imagining all sorts of catastrophes. "I don't want to hear about you dying. I hate it. I won't listen."

Damon pulled her close to his side, ignoring his clamoring relatives who pushed close to Sophie and Thag, interrogating them. "I am not leaving you," he said, "but you're not practical, my fey darling, and I intend to see to your welfare. Even if I die before we marry, you will still have twenty percent of my holdings."

"Stop, please stop." Zen squeezed her eyes shut, trying to wipe out a suddenly vivid picture of Damon trapped under the wheels of a truck.

"Darling." Damon pushed her a little away from him and stared down at her stricken face. "Darling, I'm sorry. I didn't mean to upset you." He ran his index finger down her nose. "Where has your down-to-earth common sense gone?"

"It drowned in the Irish Sea," she mumbled, letting her arms slip around his waist for a moment before she pushed away from him and turned to watch the others. "Why are they so concerned that your mother is marrying Thag?" she asked. "I should think they would be happy for her. He doesn't want her money."

"I should think not." Damon gave a hard laugh. "He could buy and sell anyone here tonight—except me." His hand settled at her waist, where he stroked her gently.

"Then why do Sandor and Dalia look so sour?"

"Because my mother has been supporting them for years—even though they have money of their own. My dear aunt and cousin do not believe in spending their own capital if they can sponge off my mother. She allows it, though she knows I disapprove. Thag will put a stop to it, and they know that, too."

"Good. I hope she marries him tomorrow," Zen said with conviction.

Damon laughed, then raised his voice. "Mother, my future wife says she wishes you would marry Thag tomorrow."

"Damon, for God's sake!" Zen felt weak with embarrassment as every eye in the room fixed on her.

"Do you, Xenobia?" Sophie sounded like a breathless schoolgirl.

Zen's gaze moved from one guest to the other and finally settled on Thag, who looked unnaturally pale. But despite his obvious unease, he stood protectively close to Sophie, and Zen was struck anew by what a kind and caring man he was. He would make Sophie a faithful husband, a loyal defender, and a charming companion.

"Yes," Zen said, "I would like it very much if you married Thag—soon, so the boys will have a grandfather."

Sophie's eyes widened. "I hadn't thought of that. Yes, the boys do love you, Thag. We will get the license tomorrow."

Pythagoras let out a deep breath and kissed Sophie's cheek. "Tomorrow we will be the first in line at the license bureau."

"Ridiculous!" exclaimed Dalia, trying to take hold of her sister's arm. "Let me talk to you."

"No," Zen said loudly, surprising herself. "You've talked too much already. They'll be married as soon as possible, and the boys will attend the ceremony."

Dalia assessed Zen with deep contempt. "Your sister Eleni was never so bold."

A mutinous look came over Sophie's face. "Many times you caused Davos and Eleni unhappiness, Dalia," she said. "They loved each other so much, yet you hurt my daughter-in-law by saying unkind, spiteful things." Sophie glanced at Zen. "You have been unkind to Xenobia as well."

Zen's instinct to protect her loved ones—whether alive or just remembered—rose to the fore, and she stepped toward Dalia with deadly menace in her step. "If I had known you hurt Eleni—" Suddenly two iron-hard arms came around her chest, knocking the breath out of her.

Damon's warm breath grazed her cheek before his firm lips nuzzled her neck. "Watch out for my tiger, Aunt Dalia," he warned, chuckling. "She bites."

Dalia sniffed disdainfully and stomped away.

Gradually, in desultory fashion, members of the family began to take their leave. Unlike Dalia and Sandor, some smiled and wished the newly engaged couple sincerely well in their new life together.

When Sandor took Zen's hand and lifted it to his mouth, Damon was there to free Zen's hand and glower at his cousin.

"A simple handshake will do, Sandor," he said.

"You were always possessive of your toys."

His words inflamed Zen. "I'm no one's toy, Sandor." She, too, gave him a dark, warning look.

"Good night, Aunt Dalia." Damon smiled at his stern-faced aunt.

"I hope you know what you're getting into, Damon." Without another word she swept past Zen into the huge foyer and out of the house.

"Your family—" Zen began angrily, immediately mollified when Damon's arm circled her waist. His laughter tickled the hair on her neck.

Zen broke away from his embrace and turned to say good night to Sophie and Thag, who were sitting on the settee. They were staring into each other's eyes, awed expressions on their faces. Zen smiled fondly. It was lovely to see two people so much in love.

Feeling somewhat sentimental, and in no mood to confront Damon, Zen hoped to slip upstairs while he was giving Yanos instructions about how to store the remaining bottles of unopened champagne.

She had climbed the stairs and reached the sanctuary of her room when the door opened and closed behind her. She turned to see Damon, a determined look on his face. "Now, Damon, I already said that I would not sleep with you while—"

"Love." He held up both hands, palms out. "I haven't come to coerce you. I just thought you would like your ring. After all, it *was* your engagement party."

"Oh, I forgot."

"Did you?" He smiled lazily, but his eyes burned with a light she had seen all too often.

"What I mean is, I don't need—"

"No, don't say anything. Not about this." In an instant he was at her side, enfolding her in his arms. "I want to give you the world." He reached into his pocket, pulled out a box, and flicked open the lid.

An exquisite marquise diamond lay on apricot-colored velvet. Zen gasped. It was beautiful. But far too precious for her.

She gulped. "I'd be afraid to wear it."

"If you don't, I'll give it away," Damon said, pushing it onto her finger, then lifting her hand to his mouth.

Zen reeled. "Don't talk like that."

"Then don't say you won't wear it." He stared moodily down at her. "Do you like it?"

"Very much. Especially the gold filigree setting. It looks like an heirloom."

"It should. It belonged to my grandmother Aristides."

"It did?" Zen's hand jerked out of his. "But it must be so valuable. Are you sure it's safe to wear it?"

"I asked the jeweler that when he sized it for you. He checked all the points."

"How?"

Damon didn't pretend not to know what she was asking. "How did I get your ring size?" He smiled. "I enlisted Lona's help. I asked her to watch and see if you ever left your school ring on your dresser." He shrugged. "You did. I measured it, and Lona returned it for me."

"Sneaky, aren't you?" Zen held up her hand to the light.

"With you I have to be." He growled into her hair. "Do I get a thank you kiss?"

She hesitated. "I suppose so." She glanced up as his mouth descended to hers, raising her index finger between them. "But I can't sleep with—"

Damon bit her finger. "For God's sake, woman, don't tell me again that you aren't sleeping with me. I don't like hearing it." His mouth took hers with heart-melting tenderness, his tongue a gentle probe between her lips. "I do love to kiss you," he muttered against her mouth. She was lost to him.

"I like it, too," Zen murmured, letting her body mold itself to his.

"Lord, Zen, don't do that. I'll be in the shower all night."

She laughed. She felt as light as a balloon and as

powerful as an Amazon. Her skin tingled. She was going to marry him, the man she had loved since she was twenty years old! It was too good to be true.

Yes, far too good to be real, a cynical side of herself argued. Dreams didn't come true. They died slowly, a lingering death.

Whatever Damon felt for her—and she doubted it was love—was bound to change, probably sooner rather than later.

Damon groaned and stepped away from her, not hiding his arousal. "Zen, I'm not used to this—and I damn well don't like it. Good night!" He pivoted on his heel and left the room.

Zen had felt as if she were floating on a pink cloud, but now she landed with a bump. "Do you mean you're not used to denying yourself sex?" she demanded of the closed door. "How dare you be unfaithful to me!" Her anger grew threefold as she imagined him chuckling with a blond . . . no, a redhead . . . no, a stately brunette. "I'll cut him out of my heart before he cuts me out of his life," she decided.

All at once a wave of fatigue assailed her. It had been an exhausting and emotionally draining day.

She washed her face and climbed into bed, cradling her cheek in her left hand and falling almost immediately into the black well of sleep.

The next day Sophie and Thag took the boys with them to the courthouse and obtained a marriage license. They returned to announce that they would marry a few days later. Zen shared their joy. Sophie's obvious happiness made her see her future mother-in-law in a new light.

The wedding was simple and small, attended only by David, Daniel, Zen, and Damon. When they returned to the house, they enjoyed a special dinner prepared by Maria and served by Lona and Yanos, who were all encouraged to join the toast with vintage champagne.

"Are we drinking champagne, Aunt Zeno?" Daniel

quizzed, watching the bubbles in his glass.

"No, dear, you're drinking sparkling grape juice. Do you like it?"

He nodded and edged next to her on the settee. He leaned his head on her arm.

Concerned, Zen raised his chin in her hand and studied his face. "What is it, dear? Aren't you feeling well?"

"Yes ... I mean I'm fine." Daniel's voice faltered.

"Tell me. What's wrong?"

His lip quavered before he bit down on it. "Aunt Dalia said ... she said that you and Nonna won't want me and David when you get married." Daniel's eyes filled with tears.

"My own boy," Zen cried, enfolding him close to her, her face pressed against his head.

"What is it? What's wrong?" David climbed up on Zen's lap, wanting to be hugged, too.

"My babies ..." Zen was so full of feeling that she couldn't say anything else.

The three of them sat locked in a tight embrace for long, emotion-filled moments.

Damon glanced at them from where he stood with Maria, Yanos, and Lona and strode immediately over to them. He sank to his knees in front of them. "All right, what's going on here?" he demanded.

"Your aunt Dalia told Daniel that your mother and I wouldn't want the boys after we were married." Zen reached for a tissue to dry her eyes.

"Such big tears on your cheek, love. Ummm, salty too," Damon crooned. Then he turned to the boys and held their gazes with his own. "Nonna and Thag will be going on a trip soon," he explained, "but they will be back before Zen and I get married. When we go away for our trip, they will stay here with you. When we come back, all of us—David, Daniel, Aunt Zeno, and I—will be going on a trip together. Then the four of us will come back here to live. We're a family now. We'll be together."

"Then Aunt Dalia was wrong?" David asked, sighing.

Damon nodded. "Aunt Dalia was very wrong."

Both boys smiled, then slid from Zen's lap and ran to their grandmother and their new grandfather, talking at full speed. The indulgent adults hovered over them.

"And you," Damon continued, still kneeling in front of Zen, "must stop jumping to conclusions. Come to me if something is wrong. We'll settle it together." He rose, pulling her up with him. "We'll be married in one week— in nine days, to be exact, and then all your ghosts will go away."

Amazed, Zen looked up at him. He could see into her heart of hearts. He had opened the door that no one had ever opened, the door that concealed her most private fears. He seemed able to recognize and fulfill her needs before she recognized them herself.

While Sophie and Thag went on their short wedding trip, Zen was thrust into prewedding chaos. She had expected to shop for a dress; she had not expected a phone call from a designer named Charine, who informed her that her showroom was located on Madison near Sixtieth Street and to ask if Thursday morning would be suitable for the first fittings.

"Fittings?" Zen repeated, waving frantically at Damon, who had entered the room. She held her hand over the phone and explained who was at the other end.

He nodded and took the phone from her. "Charine? Damon Aristides. Yes, fine . . . Right. I'll bring her in myself. Yes." He replaced the receiver. "I have to get some work done anyway. I'll leave you at the showroom. Then when you're ready you can come to the office. I'll send my driver to pick you up."

"You will?" Zen was amazed. "But you'll be busy."

"Yes. I generally am . . . and lately I've taken off more time than ever before. But I have a very efficient staff." Damon shrugged and kissed her open mouth. "Don't look so surprised, love. The boss should be able to play hooky now and then."

"Yes," she agreed, bemused.

Damon frowned. "Perhaps you would prefer another designer. I should have remembered your own designing talents. Would you rather design you own dress, love?"

Zen considered for a moment and shook her head. "I'll probably have a few ideas of my own, but I know and admire Charine's work."

"Good." Damon kissed her again. "I just came in to say good-bye. I have a meeting at eleven."

Thursday was a drizzly day with a bite to the misty wind. Zen was content to cuddle close to Damon during the ride into Manhattan, glad that they were being chauffeured.

Damon dropped her at the designer's, after explaining that he wouldn't come in with her. He had piles of work to go through.

Charine was a small, birdlike woman with coal black hair that she wore twisted into a chignon. From her Italian leather shoes to the diamond studs in her ears she gave off an aura of French chic.

To Zen's surprise, the first order of the day was to provide her with nightwear.

"This was Madame Aristides' idea," Charine explained, smiling. "She informed me that you are to have silk in golds and greens that complement your coloring." Charine studied Zen as she stood before her in bra and briefs. "Madame was right. Those colors are good for you." She snapped her fingers, and an iridescent garment was placed in her hands, a pale gold silk kaftan that fell full from the shoulders. The front closed with two tiny hooks.

Zen tried it on, and a tiny smile appeared on Charine's face.

"Ah, good," She turned Zen in front of the three-way mirror in the large fitting room. "See for yourself."

Zen's eyes widened at the sight of the transparent fabric, which rippled on her form like a silken waterfall. "It's beautiful."

"Your husband will lose his mind," Charine predicted, fully satisfied.

Zen lost track of the garments she put on. He~ head was filled with silks, woolens, and linens.

Finally Charine brought her the wedding dress. Zen took one look at the ruffles and balked. "No. I look better in tailored clothes," she said. Nothing would dissuade her. "It has too many ruffles for me."

Charine sighed and tapped one finger on her chin, then snapped her fingers. "Bring the special one—the cream satin," she told the assistant.

The pale cream satin had thin straps and no other decoration. The bustline was defined by stitching, but the dress fell to a demi-train that was plain and unadorned.

When Zen put it on, the designer and her assistants inhaled sharply. "You look like a miniature Venus. Though you are tiny of stature, mademoiselle, you have poise. And you are right about the dress. I will add sleeves—long and tight to the wrist," Charine mused. "And the neckline shall be square with the shoulders barely covered and the back falling to a deep V. It shall be stark—your hair, the gold-red color, and pink pearls in the ears shall be your only adornment. Five white flowers will tie back your hair so that it cascades down you back like a veil." Charine's eyes snapped in creative fervor. "You will be a goddess."

"I'll settle for making it down the aisle without falling," Zen said, smiling weakly as Charine buzzed around her like a queen bee, tucking, nipping, straightening, grumbling to herself.

"What? What did you say? Oh . . . ha, the American joke. How droll."

Not all of Zen's protestations that she really wasn't a clothes horse, despite her work in fashion, convinced Charine that she didn't need all the clothes and lingerie that an assistant jotted down in a loose-leaf notebook.

"Well, it is done, Mademoiselle Driscoll. The dress will be ready in plenty of time. Monsieur Aristides assures me that no expense must be spared." Charine smiled at Zen.

"But I won't wear half of these things," Zen protested.

Charine shrugged. "But it will be such a comfort to know that they are there to discard." Charine herself accompanied Zen to the front entrance of the showroom and bowed her out to the waiting Rolls-Royce.

"That must be the logic that sends such a large number of Americans to bankruptcy proceedings," Zen muttered, sitting back against the plush cushions.

Slowly they made their way through Manhattan traffic. Brakes screeched; horns blasted. Finally they pulled up in front of Olympus Ltd, managing to beat a Mercedes Benz into a parking space.

The chauffeur opened Zen's door, ignoring the fist-shaking driver of the Mercedes.

Zen, too, ignored the man's invective. She was about to identify herself to the security man on duty when he bowed to her and led her to an elevator.

"Mr. Aristides has been calling down every fifteen minutes for the last hour," the man explained in a Brooklyn accent. "I've worked for the boss for a few years and never remember him gettin' in such a whirl over a woman." He smiled at Zen as she entered the elevator. "Just punch the button. Take ya right there."

Zen's stomach and knees met in the tingling, rapid ascent.

When the doors opened, Damon was standing there. He pulled her from the elevator into his arms. His mouth came down over hers.

Immediately her limbs grew weak, and her thoughts whirled away. Damon filled all her senses. "People will see," she managed to gasp, trying to force her eyes open.

"Darling, you're in my private office," Damon explained, pulling her over to his desk and sitting down with her in his lap. I've been thinking about you all day, haven't been able to concentrate on the Rothman Cable problem at all."

"Business first," Zen croaked, clutching at his shoulders, rubbing her head against his chin.

"Tell me what—" A red light blinked on the desk

console. Damon glowered. He punched a button. "Yes?"

"I'm sorry, Mr. Aristides, but Miss Crawford insisted. She says she is only in town for—"

Damon barked into the speaker, then broke the connection.

Zen watched, fascinated, as his face darkened to crimson. She was sure he had forgotten her, even though she was sitting on his lap.

Who was Miss Crawford that the mere mention of her name provoked such an immediate embarrassed response from him? Were they involved? Did Damon love her? Zen shook her head to clear it of the black thoughts that crowded it.

Chapter 8

THE WEDDING DAY dawned gray and drizzly. It perfectly matched Zen's mood. She and Damon had been walking a tightrope for the last three days—ever since she had demanded to know who Miss Crawford was.

At first Damon had hedged. Then finally, infuriated by her needling, he'd told her.

"All right, dammit, she was my mistress. But I haven't seen her in six months." He had stood before Zen, fists clenched.

She took several deep breaths. She felt as though a truck had just rammed her middle. "So, in the meantime you found a substitute—me," she accused. "But now your West Coast sweetie wants you back. Is that it?"

"No, that is not it." Damon's body tensed with anger. "And don't jump to any—"

"Don't you swear at me," Zen retorted, her hands on her hips.

"I'm not swearing at you." Damon ground his teeth.

"Don't you raise your voice either, because I won't

let you push me around." Zen drew herself up to her full five feet two inches and glared at him.

Damon gazed down at her, his chest heaving. "Just damn well remember that we're getting married in three days." He stormed from the room. The door banged shut behind him, the sound reverberating through the house.

"Womanizer!" Zen called after him. "I never cry, I never cry," she murmured to herself, very fast and restlessly pacing the room. "Well, hardly ever," she amended. She held a hand to her mouth as shudders wracked her body.

Now, on her wedding day, Zen stared out the window at a gray Long Island Sound. "I should take the boys and skip town," she said to herself as she gathered sweet-smelling soaps and shampoos for her bath.

As she lathered her body and hair, she imagined herself with the two boys in a giant balloon crossing the United States, then on camels traversing the Sahara Desert, then in a three-man sailboat braving the Pacific. She would just disappear, she thought as she spread lotion on her body, then donned the filmy panties and stockings that would be her only undergarments. The heavy satin gown was lined with the softest cotton.

Sighing, Zen let Lona drop the gown over her head just as Sophie walked into the room. The older woman sighed, too, and folded her hands in front of her as she watched Lona arrange the garland of white roses at the back of Zen's head. "Charine told me you would look like a goddess from Olympus and you do, child," she said. "Eleni was lovely, but you are beautiful."

Zen swallowed. "Thank you, Mrs. Aristides."

"Can you not call me Sophie now?"

"Yes, of course. If you like." Zen felt uncomfortable under Sophie's soft gaze.

Lona turned Zen around so that she was facing the three-way mirror. She sucked in her breath. She had never looked better. The pearl studs in her ears seemed to have the same pink sheen as her skin. Her hair was like golden fire. The skin above her breasts was almost the same creamy color as the dress.

She picked up the one long-stemmed white rose that she would carry and felt something hard in the nylon net hand holder. She pushed aside the ruching. An emerald pin in the shape of a shamrock!

"There's an inscription on the back," Sophie said, smiling.

"My sweet luck. Damon," the inscription read, making Zen's eyes fill.

"Lona, leave us," Sophie said imperiously. "I wish to speak to Xenobia alone."

"But, madame . . ." Lona frowned, and glanced at the clock.

"It's all right, it's all right. I will not make her late. Father Constantine will wait, regardless, and the judge is a friend of Damon's."

Zen watched as Sophie followed Lona to the door and shut it behind her. She braced herself.

Sophie turned. "Do not be alarmed, child. I have no intention of attacking you. But I do want to apologize." She took a deep breath. "Three years ago, I let my sister chase you away. Because I was afraid, I suppose, but whatever the reason, I regret it. I caused you . . . and my beloved son . . . much pain. You see, I saw how much in love with you he was."

Zen was speechless. "That's not possible."

"Yes, child, he was in love with you—so much so that, when you left to live in Ireland, my Damon became someone clse, someone hard, cynical, often unkind, often cruel. Although he was never dishonest, he became ruthless. You had been gone two years when I finally came to accept that what he felt for you was great and all-consuming. The feeling had turned inside him like a Judas blade, destroying him."

Sophie's eyes shone with unshed tears. "I recalled how he had been with you in the beginning . . . how he had laughed, how open and alive he'd been. Because you were gone from him, he had hidden his feelings behind a locked door." She pursed her lips "His advcn-

tures with women were chronicled in too many period-
icals."

"I . . . I saw some of the write-ups in the American
papers I received in Dublin," Zen admitted.

"Lord, that son of mine. Even in Athens—" Sophie
shook her head and fell silent. "Finally Thag convinced
me that Damon was pining for you."

"No," Zen whispered, though a faint ray of hope was
dawning. She tried to tamp it down.

"Yes. That is when I decided to convince you to come
home again. That and the desire to see my David as well.
I hurt you both, and for that I am most sorry."

"It wasn't your fault. Damon and I are too volatile
together."

"Yes, you are that," Sophie concurred. "But you are
also good for each other. I have heard Damon laugh
again, seen him come alive. He is once more eager to
enjoy all that life has to offer. I have seen you. You love
my son—as you loved him once before."

"No," Zen whispered, "I love him much more now."

"Oh, dear." Sophie smiled. "That could be very dangerous for Damon, couldn't it?"

Zen's face flushed with embarrassment. "I don't know
what's the matter with me. I'm such a klutz when he's
around me."

"The boys told me that Damon read them the story
of the albatross, the bird that brought bad luck when the
mariner killed it. I see a parallel between that story and
your own. Fortune smiled on you and Damon when you
first fell in love. It was only after you denied that love
and separated that you both became so unhappy. It's only
when you are fighting that love, instead of accepting it
in your heart, that you have these accidents." Sophie
chuckled. "I am sure that soon you will be handling my
son with ease."

"Never with ease." Zen grimaced ruefully, and Sophie
laughed.

"Come, my child, say that you forgive me. My son
must be growing impatient. He told me you would not

let him near you while I was in the house."

Zen lowered her eyes. "He shouldn't have said that."

"Ah, but it was so good to have Damon come and talk to me about you. Instead of the cold man who would not answer my questions, he is once again a loving son."

"He's still a blabbermouth."

Sophie laughed again, and Zen felt a smile pull at her mouth. She stretched and kissed the older woman's cheek. "I forgive you . . . and I thank you for Daniel. He is a beautiful boy."

Just then someone banged on the door, startling them both.

"Zen, for God's sake, hurry."

Sophie looked at Zen, her eyes brimming with mirth. "I think the bridegroom has lost what little patience he had."

"He won't wait for anything." Zen took a deep breath, wanting to believe what Sophie had told her but not able to heal all her deeply buried wounds in an instant.

"Oh, by the way, Xenobia, there is an Irishman downstairs who says he is a friend of yours."

"Seamus! He came!" Zen clapped her hands in delight as Sophie nodded that that was the name he had given— Seamus Dare.

"Is my mother there with you?" Damon demanded, rattling the doorknob.

"Yes," Sophie answered, opening the door. "But you cannot come in. Go downstairs and watch your bride descend to join you."

"Tell her to hurry. The guests are getting anxious," Damon said.

"Pooh," his mother responded. "You are the one who is growing anxious." Sophie looked back at Zen. "I am glad the priest will marry you."

Zen heard Damon's disgruntled voice fading as he returned to the small gathering who would witness the ceremony. Three times the number would join them for the reception.

Zen checked her appearance in the mirror, feeling a

momentary sadness because her other Irish friends couldn't be there. Still she was glad that Seamus had come all this way to toast her new life.

There was another knock on the door as she was about to leave the room. She was ready to tell Damon that the groom should not see the bride before the ceremony. But when she opened the door, she was enveloped in a huge hug.

"Seamus," she breathed.

"Did you think I would miss this, colleen?" The sound of his Irish brogue brought tears to her eyes. She had such wonderful friends in Dublin. Would she ever see them again?

"I've come to see that rapscallion, David."—Seamus kissed her nose—"Not to see you." He leaned away from her, still clasping her arms. "Not that you aren't passing pretty today." He kissed her again as they both walked to the top of the stairs, where they stood in full sight of the assembled group.

Damon was standing there with the boys, Father Constantine, and the judge.

David caught sight of them. "Seamus!" he called out, then clamped a hand over his mouth as Aunt Dalia shushed him.

"I've decided that I will give the bride away," Seamus told Zen, his eyes twinkling. "That will give that fulminating giant something to think about."

"He may kill you." Zen warned, but she took his proffered arm, feeling the need of his assistance.

They descended the stairs together, as the processional began.

Zen kept her eyes straight ahead, smiling a little when she heard Daniel whisper, "Aunt Zeno sure is pretty."

When she stopped next to Damon, Seamus kissed her on the cheek and stepped to one side.

She looked up at Damon, but his eyes were fixed on Seamus.

Father Constantine cleared his throat several times before he was able to catch Damon's attention. "Join hands, please," he intoned.

Zen felt her hand being taken, felt Damon's life force pumping into her blood.

She made her responses in a low voice. Damon answered strong and sure... the way he did everything.

When he turned her toward him, she felt as light as air and filled with joy. Her hand rested on his cheek as he lifted her off her feet, and his mouth found hers and lingered there.

Then people were crowding around them, congratulating them with exuberant hugs and exclamations. Damon was forced to release Zen. Well-wishers kissed her cheek. Seamus kissed her mouth.

"You're just trying to start something," Zen chided him, then grinned when David tackled him around the knees.

Seamus was about to swing the boy into the air when all at once he paused, staring at someone behind David. "So... and you must be Daniel. And a fine broth of a boy you are with such a name." Seamus kept hold of David's hand as he held out the other to Daniel. "And I'm your Uncle Seamus."

Zen's smile faltered as she looked up at Damon and saw the grim expression on his face. His black eyes were on Seamus. Then, even as she watched, a stunning woman, tall and dark, slipped her hand through Damon's arm, commanding his attention.

"Damon, darling, you must introduce me to your... ah... cute little wife." She turned to Zen. "I'm Cherry Crawford. Damon and I have been close for years."

Zen didn't hear what Damon said to the woman. A roaring in her ears and a red haze in front of her eyes deafened and blinded her.

Then Sophie was at her side. "Xenobia, dear, you must meet the Levinsons. She was Marta Leandros, and we went to school together." She plucked at Zen's sleeve. "She has brought you a set of Haviland china. I know you're so partial to dishes." Soohie's eyes darted nervously from Zen to Damon and back again.

"I am?" Zen stared blankly at her mother-in-law, then patted her arm.

"Sophie." Thag appeared at his wife's side. "Don't worry. Zen is not worried." But his frown conveyed his own concern.

With great effort Zen smiled at her mother-in-law, masking an anger that threatened to overwhelm her. How dare Damon invite his former mistress to the wedding! But out loud she said, "Thag is right. I'm not upset."

Sophie closed her eyes in dismay. "I couldn't believe it when I saw her walk into the room and take a seat. Dalia had pointed her out to me many times before, so I knew her."

Just then Seamus broke away from Damon and Cherry and returned to Zen, who introduced him to Sophie and Thag. "Shall I take the luscious Cherry away while you receive your guests?" he suggested.

"Would you?" Sophie gave him a grateful smile.

"Perhaps she would like to receive with us," Zen whispered sarcastically to Thag.

He bit his lip and agreed, "That would be interesting."

Damon strode toward them, his eyes narrowed on Seamus. "You seem to be everywhere my wife is."

"And you seem to be everywhere Ms. Crawford is," Seamus observed.

Damon seemed to swell with indignation.

"Mr. Dare," Sophie interjected, "has offered to accompany Ms. Crawford through the reception line."

"Fine," Damon snapped.

"Delighted, ma'am," Seamus said at the same time. He grinned at Zen and winked, then reached for Cherry's hand and tucked it into his arm. "C'mon along, my lovely. You just got lucky, as you Yankees say."

"Really?" Cherry drawled, her smile not quite reaching her eyes as she touched Damon's arm. "We'll talk later, darling—when we're alone."

Zen reeled. Stars, wheels, and big dots floated in front of her eyes.

For a moment, as she and Damon moved toward the arch of white orchids that led to the dining room, Zen had to resist the urge to heave the tiered wedding cake at her husband. "How dare you do that?" she demanded.

"What the hell are you talking about?" They stood grim-faced under the arch. Sophie and Thag stood to one side and began to form a receiving line that led into the dining room.

"Don't swear at me, you womanizer," Zen snapped.

"Womanizer!" Damon exclaimed. "Will you kindly explain what you mean by that? And where the hell did that Irish rover come from? Why was he up in your room?"

"Seamus Dare is my friend and a man of honor." Her voice softened as she addressed Daniel. "Yes, dear, you and David come stand with us."

"Friend!" Damon's voice rose. His mother leaned forward and shot him a warning glance.

"Seamus and I—" Zen began hotly, then lowered her voice as Daniel looked up at her. She smiled and leaned closer to Damon, speaking in a harsh whisper.

"Seamus and I have never lived together."

"That's what you're telling me. I saw the way he looked at you as you came down the stairs with him."

"Don't try to weasel out of—oh, yes, Mrs. Dinmont. Damon has spoken of you often. Thank you. Yes, how do you do?" Zen's head began to spin as dozens of guests greeted her. Damon played the charming host at her side, but Zen sensed the lingering tension in him.

Long before everyone had arrived, David grew bored greeting guests. "Aunt Zeno, Curly is thirsty." He leaned around Damon's legs and gazed out the window at the lawn that swept down to the water. "I better go give him a drink. All right?" His hopeful look was mirrored in Daniel's face.

Zen was about to tell them that they could play on the terrace when Damon said, "You may go outside, but you cannot go down to the water or throw sticks for Curly that might go into the water. Is that clear?"

Both boys nodded enthusiastically.

"Stay in sight of this window," Damon cautioned, his voice brooking no disobedience.

"We will, Uncle Damon," they said in unison. They pushed open the French doors and skipped out onto the terrace.

"I should have insisted they change their clothes." Zen winced as David climbed the low concrete balustrade that circled the terrace.

Damon shrugged. "They need the fresh air more than they do a wedding reception. Besides, if I know Yanos, he's out there somewhere watching for them. He won't let them get into too much trouble."

"No." Zen smiled up at Damon, then remembered that she was angry with him. She looked away.

"I want to know more about Seamus Dare," he said, his arm tightening around her. "I thought he was older, not so close to you in age."

"I will be glad to answer any of your questions—if you will tell me why Cherry Crawford was invited to our wedding."

"Cherry wasn't invited—at least not by me."

"Hah! Do you think I'm a fool?"

"You're a fool if you think I would invite my . . . that is . . ."

"Do go on. You were about to say 'my mistress,' I believe."

"Damn you, Zen! You know I wouldn't invite her to our wedding."

"How do I know that? She called you at the office when I was there, and you forgot all about me."

"It would be pretty damn hard to forget you when you argue and fight with me all the time."

Zen felt a sharp pain at his words. "I . . . I . . . we don't fight all the time."

"Most of the time. And I'm sick of it. I don't want any more of it. You know damn well that I would never invite—"

"Damon, dear," Cherry Crawford called, "do tell me what you wanted when you rang me a week ago. I called your office, but someone was with you and you couldn't talk." Cherry glided up to them, her black silk suit clinging to her. She turned to Zen. "I hope I haven't offended you by wearing black to your wedding, dear, but I am in mourning of a sort, you know. I even have black undies on, Damon." She smiled up at him, then back at Zen. "You understand, of course."

Suddenly the situation struck Zen as incredibly funny. She couldn't contain her laughter as she told Cheery, "Yes, I think I do understand. My husband must have had his hands full with you."

"I did." Damon's answering chuckle sent a warm tingle down Zen's spine.

Cherry's doelike eyes narrowed in suspicion.

"I think what my wife is saying is that she knows I didn't invite you to the wedding, Cherry," Damon explained quietly. He reached out to clasp Zen to his side, and his mouth brushed the top of her head in a tender caress.

Seamus ambled over to them. "Come, my lovely. Soon the musicians will begin playing." He shook a finger at Cherry. "I could have told you it would be most foolish to spar with Zenny Driscoll."

"Zen Aristides," Damon corrected, glowering.

"Xenobia Driscoll Aristides," Zen amended firmly, her eyes darting between them.

Damon's hard gaze was locked on Seamus. Then, to Zen's surprise, his expression gradually softened, and he chuckled. A mischievous twinkle crept into Seamus's eyes, and he clapped Damon on the back.

"Women," he exclaimed and let out a boisterous laugh.

"Women," Damon agreed in a spirit of hearty male camaraderie.

He swooped down to give Zen a resounding kiss and walked off with Seamus, talking with him like an old friend.

Zen stared after them in stupefied amazement. Then a family friend claimed her attention.

Much later, after she and Damon had cut the cake, dancing began in the spacious solarium, which offered a sweeping view of the Sound. Potted flowers, all white, had been banked around the five-piece orchestra.

As their guests drifted through the spacious rooms, Damon and Zen found themselves alone for a moment.

Zen fed Damon a piece of cake from her plate. "So you're a pantie collector, are you? And do you like black in particular?"

Damon held her wrist as he nibbled the cake, then nipped at her skin. "I admit to having a bent for sensual things, and I like all colors, especially if you're wearing them. If you should ever want me to chase you around the grounds before removing your underthings, I accept the challenge." Damon leered at her. "In fact, just imagining it is having an effect on me. Shall I send the guests home?"

Zen laughed, feeling both powerfully sexy and deliciously weak. "We can't do—" she whirled toward the French doors. "Where are the boys? I haven't heard or seen them for quite a while." She stepped outside.

Damon followed, frowning. "Are you putting me off again?" he demanded.

"No." She had to smile at his dark expression. "You look just like David and Daniel when you do that."

Damon took hold of her arm, stopping her, then stripped off his silk jacket and draped it over her shoulders. "There's still a nip in the air, and too much of you is showing," he explained, holding the jacket closed in front of her. He leaned down to kiss her. "You're mine, Mrs. Aristides."

"Driscoll Aristides," Zen insisted.

"Is that so important to you?"

"What?" Zen couldn't suppress a grin. Damon chuckled, and kissed her. "Let's go find the boys."

Hand in hand, they crossed the lawn. As she gazed up at Damon and he returned her tender gaze, Zen felt filled to bursting with happiness. But as the minutes went on and the boys didn't answer their calls, she began to worry.

When she caught sight of Yanos heading toward the water, also calling for them, she sucked in a shaky breath.

"Zen, stop it." Damon pulled her around to face him. "Don't start imagining things. I'm sure they're all right."

"Yes, but we have to find them, see them."

Damon hailed Yanos and strode over to him. Zen stumbled after him, impeded by her satin sandals.

Damon turned to face her. "Go back to the house. Yanos and I—"

"No!" Zen shook her head, stubbornly determined to stay and help.

He shook his head but didn't protest further and followed Yanos to the carriage house.

Zen headed instinctively toward the water. Something seemed to be pulling her there.

Suddenly she saw the boys. They were sitting in a raftlike wooden vessel, floating about a hundred yards from shore. Curly was swimming next to them, trying to push them.

Zen didn't hesitate. She threw Damon's jacket to the ground and peeled the satin wedding gown from her body, then kicked off her shoes.

"Damon!" she called once, then began wading out into the icy water, forcing herself to disregard her numb arms and legs.

Curly was making a valiant effort, but Zen could tell that he was tiring. Though the boys weren't far from shore now, if Curly let up on his struggles, the flimsy craft would drift away, pulled by unseen currents.

The water had reached Zen's breastbone when a hand suddenly caught her arm. "Go back, Zenny. I'll get them," Seamus said at her side.

"Oh, Seamus, I'm so glad to see you. It may take two of us to bring them in."

Before Seamus could reply, Damon bellowed from shore, "Damn you, Zen, I could throttle you! Get back here this instant. Are you trying to kill yourself?"

She glanced back to see Damon stripping off his shirt and shoes. In a flash he was plowing through the water in a powerful crawl. She watched, treading water, as he reached the boys and began pulling the raft toward shore.

Without speaking, awash in relief, Zen turned around and headed back, sure that the boys were now safe. She stumbled onto dry land, shivering, and was vaguely aware that blankets were being wrapped around her and Seamus. But her eyes were fixed on Damon and the twins as he lifted them from the raft and into the blankets Maria and Lona held ready.

Zen rushed over to them, oblivious to all else. "Don't you ever do that again," she scolded even as she drew them into a fierce embrace. She sniffed and hurried after them as Damon whisked them across the lawn, into the house, and up the stairs.

Sophie stood in the foyer, wringing her hands and whispering over and over, "Thank God, thank God."

Damon dissuaded Zen from giving the boys their bath. Instead, he left them in the servants' capable care and led Zen to his own apartment, where he ran a tub of hot water.

"But are you sure Lona and Maria will watch them?" Zen asked as she sank to her chin in the soothing water. "Oh, Damon, I blame myself for not watching them."

He stripped the clothes from his own body, his eyes never leaving her. "Yanos blames himself, Lona blames herself. My mother is filled with guilt." He sank down next to her in the spacious tub and folded her close. She closed her eyes in utter bliss, letting the water lap over and calm her. "The boys have lived here together for several weeks and haven't disobeyed," Damon went on. "This time they did disobey and they will be punished for it. They were using the top of the old cistern for a raft. Yanos had put it on a pile of junk to be burned. The boys found it and decided to play Huckleberry Finn. That's it. It's all over."

Damon massaged Zen's warming body, arousing an even deeper heat. "Boys do crazy things," he mused. "It's the part of them that tells them to assert themselves, rebel, accept any challenge. If a boy survives a wild boyhood, he can survive anything."

"Do mothers of boys survive?" Zen mumbled against his throat.

"Only sometimes." Damon chuckled.

"Did you ever use this tub with Cherry?" Zen asked faintly.

"No woman has ever shared these rooms with me—and no one ever will, except you."

"You had an apartment in town?"

"A penthouse in Manhattan, yes," he answered. "I won't lie to you, Zen. When we were apart, there were many women, all sizes, all shapes, all—"

"Twaddle. You only had tall, gorgeous creatures with big breasts and long legs," Zen grumbled, pulling at the hair on his chest.

He laughed. "It's true that none of them was as small as you."

"You love tall women."

"No doubt I thought so once."

"Now you have a short woman. Short women are out of style."

"Good. Then I won't have to beat the men off with a stick."

Zen giggled. "There weren't many men."

"Some, though."

"Oh, yes."

There was a long silence as Damon caressed her, his hands exploring gently. "And you would have married Seamus?" he asked.

Zen realized now that it would have been a mistake to marry Seamus when her feelings for Damon were so strong. "Yes, I was leaning that way. I knew that Seamus would be good with David. He's a man of high principles, which not all his joking and easy manner hide."

"A paragon," Damon agreed ironically.

"You asked me..."

"I know what I asked you." Damon surged to his feet, pulling her with him out of the tub and into the shower stall.

"No...eek! Stop it, Damon! I hate cold showers." Zen pummeled his chest.

"All right." His expression relaxed, and he switched the water to slightly warmer. He stepped out onto the tile floor and held out a heated bath sheet for her.

"Why did you do that?" She demanded, glaring up at him.

"Caprice," he replied, his jaw tight.

"More like meanness." Zen stalked into the bedroom—and stopped dead. She had forgotten she was in Damon's wing of the house. She had no clean clothes with her.

"Your clothes are over there." Damon gestured to a long wall of cabinets in the dressing room.

"When were they moved?"

"Lona did it this morning." He held up her wedding gown. "Do you want to put this back on. Our guests will be waiting for us."

"Yes, I'll wear it." She didn't bother to tell him that she loved the dress, that she enjoyed wearing it.

They put on their clothes in comfortable silence, though several times Zen felt Damon's gaze burning into her, hot with desire. Feeling self-conscious under his probing stare, she fumbled with the tiny buttons on her gown and gratefully accepted his help when he bent to fasten them for her. He straightened in front of her, looking so handsome in his dark silk suit. When he pulled her into his arms and kissed her hard, his tongue filling her mouth, it was all she could do to remain standing. Her blood raced hot in her veins as he took her arm and led her to the top of the stairs.

They descended the grand staircase, the sounds of music, laughter, and the clink of glassware growing louder as they reached the bottom. Damon held Zen close to him. "Did I tell you that we're going to spend the night at my apartment in Manhattan?"

"Since when? I thought we had decided to stay here and take a trip later with the boys." She paused a step above him.

Damon urged her back to his side. "Yes, but we can take one night for ourselves. I've ordered a dinner to be sent there, with champagne . . ." His voice trailed off, his thoughts wandering as his eyes lingered on her red-gold hair.

"There's enough food here to feed all the starving people in Africa."

"My mother has mentioned that you are horrified by what we've spent on our guests . . . so I have had my lawyers allocate an equal amount to charity."

Zen stopped again. "What charity? Some big organization in which the money twists and winds through a bureaucratic system and only a small fraction of the original amount gets to the needy?"

Damon chuckled. "Have a little faith, wife. The money is going to build recreational facilities for the hearing-impaired, the blind, and the retarded."

He turned to stand in the foyer, one step below her. Now he was only a little taller than Zen. Her hand came up to touch his cheek.

"Thank you. That's the nicest wedding present you could have given me." Her chin trembled.

Damon sighed. "You are the least acquisitive person I have ever known. Isn't there one material thing I can give you? Please?"

"Well . . . although I do appreciate how useful the Cherokee is, it would be nice to have—"

"You're joking," Damon interrupted, throwing back his head to laugh and clutching her upper arms.

"It isn't necessary for you . . ." Zen began, puzzled.

"In the garage, at this very moment, a gold-colored Corvette is waiting for you. I was afraid to give it to you for fear you'd be angry."

Zen stared at him. He was afraid of angering her? Incredible! "A Corvette? That's some runabout. I was thinking more in terms of a VW bug or—"

Damon touched his tongue to the corner of her mouth.

"The guests will see," Zen protested, her hands tingling, her legs weakening.

"That's a very bad habit, Xenobia—always putting me off when I begin to make love to you."

"Then pick a more private place." She gave a small screech as she was swept off her feet into his arms.

Damon headed back up the stairs with powerful strides.

"Where is Uncle Damon taking you now, Aunt Zeno?"

David asked from below them in the hall. Zen twisted to see Daniel by his side, Curly and Yanos behind them. "Are you going to take a nap? I told Lona that Dan and I would like to stay up for a while. Is it all right for Yanos to meet all the people, Aunt Zeno?"

Damon paused halfway up the stairs and then returned to the foyer, letting Zen slide down his body but not releasing her. "Of course Yanos will come with you to meet the people," he said, "and you will stay close to him and Lona." He squatted down in front of the boys while Zen hovered over them, touching them, leaning down to kiss them. "You are never to do anything like that again," Damon admonished them. "Both Nonna and Aunt Zeno were very worried."

Both boys nodded, looking at Zen askance. "We won't do it again, Aunt Zeno," Daniel promised.

She nodded and gestured for them to precede her through the lounge and into the dining room. They stopped here and there to explain to people that the boys were indeed all right. "I'm fine now," she assured Aunt Sophronia, another of Damon's aunts.

"In my day girls didn't swim in cold water," said the tiny old lady. "Of course, I'm glad the boys were rescued. They are Aristides, you know." She waved her hand like Queen Victoria bestowing a blessing and moved toward the canapé tray.

Zen shook her head in exasperation. "Your family is—"

"Doesn't it make you feel good to know how important you are to them?" Damon interrupted, chuckling and hugging her to him.

"Dear Aunt Sophronia would no doubt arrange a French picnic in honor of my hanging," Zen said, watching the birdlike woman pop an entire stuffed mushroom into her mouth, then wrap some in a napkin and stow them in her capacious purse. "Why don't you give her some money, Damon? The poor dear doesn't have enough to eat."

"Aunt Sophronia is worth millions, my love. She has

a house staff of thirty. None of her investments, which are legion, has ever suffered a loss."

"But she's stealing food," Zen whispered, her eyes widening as Aunt Sophronia wended her way past trays of delicacies, selecting liberally from each of them.

"She always takes food. No one is sure what she does with it, but you can be certain it won't be wasted. Aunt Sophronia is very thrifty."

"Amazing."

Damon led Zen out onto the dance floor. As they danced, she continued to watch his aunt and to keep a wary eye on the boys. "Damon, I think she's going to take—my lord, she put a bottle of champagne in her purse!"

"And after she takes it out to her chauffeur to stash in her Rolls, she'll be back for more."

Zen looked up at him and saw no contempt or censure in his face. "You don't mind, do you?"

"Why should I mind? Aunt Sophronia supports a Boys' Club and is active in promoting rehabilitation houses for first offenders. I admire her."

Zen felt ashamed of her previous rude behavior toward the old woman. "I didn't know," she whispered as the tiny creature upended a peanut dish into her purse. As soon as she moved away, Maria refilled the dish.

Damon whirled Zen around the spacious solarium, his mouth tight, his muscles tense.

"What is it?" she asked.

"We're dancing together. We've just been married, but you, the bride, are more fascinated with the guests than with the groom." The cords in Damon's neck stood out as he stared out over her head.

Zen felt a girlish hesitancy as she looked up at him. She remembered the twenty-year-old Zen who had first worshipped Damon Aristides, and the twenty-five-year old Zen who had fled from him, brokenhearted. "I love to dance with you, Damon," she assured him.

"How do you know? We haven't danced together much," he replied sternly. Even when the heat became faster, he held her close to him and twirled sedately round the room.

"Pardon me, may I cut in?" Seamus beamed at a glowering Damon, who showed great reluctance in releasing his wife.

In seconds, Seamus and Zen were gyrating to a hot rhythm. They faced each other, not touching, but their feet and bodies moved in perfect synchronization.

When several of the guests backed away to give them more room, Seamus became more daring, his movements more complex. Zen laughed when Seamus whirled her around him, then caught her back to him in a graceful, shallow dip. Not once did her nimble-footed friend miss a beat.

When the number ended, Seamus caught Zen in his arms and planted a kiss on her mouth as the crowd laughed and applauded.

"It's time to leave." Damon all but lifted Zen free of Seamus's hold.

"So soon?" she asked, a little out of breath.

"Yes," he bit out.

Zen was about to protest, but one look at his black expression made her change her mind. "I'll go up to change my clothes," she said.

Upstairs, Lona helped her take off her gown. Her head was still buried in the depths of material when she heard the door open.

Lona was quick to slip a silken wrapper around her before Zen faced her mother-in-law. "Sophie?"

"I don't know whether to laugh or cry." Damon's mother paced restlessly up and down the spacious dressing room. "That sister of mine is filling Damon's head with foolish stories, and he is filling his mouth with whisky."

"I'll drive, don't worry," Zen assured her.

"That isn't what's worrying me, Xenobia," Sophie said. "Not that Damon will let you drive. No one drives Damon except his chauffeur, or Yanos in a pinch." She pursed her lips. "No, I'm afraid Damon might become violent. It would be most embarrassing."

"Damon is very correct in his behavior. You needn't worry." Zen zipped up the skirt of her blue Irish linen suit. Her leather shoes and bag were of the same pale color. "Did you pack everything already, Lona?" she asked.

"Damon is never civilized where you are concerned, Xenobia," Sophie said. "And it annoys me that you should continue to be so unconcerned when you husband may be downstairs fomenting chaos. Damon is terrible when he feels he is being threatened. He will attack first and ask for the full story later." Sophie raised her eyes in supplication. "I could kill that Dalia. Just because she didn't want me to marry Thag... And, of course, she knows that she cannot control you."

"How does she know that?" Zen checked her makeup for smudges.

"Damon can't control you, so how could Dalia?"

Zen knew Sophie was deeply irritated with her. "What do you want me to do?" she asked.

"Get him out of here—and do not talk to that Irishman again tonight. Not that he isn't a most charming fellow, Xenobia, but..." Sophie glanced at Lona and nodded curtly. When the woman had left the room, she added, "One of my husband's ancestors was from Mani, the region of Greece where the wild people live." Sophie nodded thoughtfully. "Sometime I see the same wildness in Damon."

Zen wanted to laugh, but Sophie's sober look stopped her. Instead, she bent to pick up her overnight case and gestured to Sophie to open the door.

As she descended the stairs again, Zen experienced a sense of déjà vu. How many times had she gone down those stairs that day?

"I don't hear any disturbing noises," she said, smiling at the older woman.

"Let's hope you can get Damon out of the house in a hurry," Sophie replied.

When they entered the living room, the first person

Zen saw was Damon, lifting a glass to his mouth and draining it. "Oh, dear," she whispered as Seamus came towards them both arms outstretched. She patted Sophie's arm. "Don't worry. No doubt Seamus wants to say good-bye. He's returning to Ireland soon."

"Not soon enough," Sophie whispered.

Zen followed the direction of her mother-in-law's gaze, and her mouth dropped open. Damon was striding angrily through the crowd, his face a hard mask. Guests stepped hastily out his way, clearing a narrow path for him.

"Damon." Zen stepped in front of him, but he lifted her like a doll and set her to one side.

Seamus looked up in surprise as Damon bore down on him. Everyone seemed turned to stone.

Zen ducked under her husband's arm and stood up, stopping him short. She reached up and pulled his stiff head down until their lips met. She let her mouth soften and move on his until she felt his response, his tongue moving to touch hers. She massaged his face and neck, and she didn't release him when she moved her mouth back an inch. "Damon, we're married," she murmured.

"I won't have him kissing you," Damon muttered back, though he didn't move away from her.

She stroked his cheek. "Seamus is a friend." She kissed him again. "People kiss their friends."

Damon straightened but kept his hands on her, kneading her shoulders, swaying imperceptibly. "Let's get out of here," he said at last, the words slightly slurred.

"Damon, if I ask for the keys to the car—because you have been drinking more than you should—what will you say? Or would you prefer having the chauffeur drive us into Manhattan?" Zen kept her voice low, for his ears only.

His mouth caressed hers. "I say I don't like it, but it's the smart thing to do." He fumbled in his jacket pocket and handed her the keys, kissed her again, then turned to speak to Sophie and Thag.

With a sigh of relief, Zen turned back to the guests and began bidding them good-bye. Damon, stiff but cordial, remained close to her side.

When it was Seamus's turn he grabbed her around the waist and kissed her full on the mouth with a noisy smack.

"Stop that, you fool," Sophie said. She tapped Seamus imperially on the arm.

Thag shook his head. "You are a wild Irishman," he said, but he, too, was smiling, and Zen couldn't help grinning in return. Seamus would keep the family well entertained during his visit.

Zen was still chuckling over something Seamus had told her as she followed Damon out to the Ferrari. Yanos was just slamming the lid of the trunk shut, having stowed away their luggage.

The old Greek rolled his eyes toward the front seat, where Damon slouched on the passenger side. "He is more in the wine than he should be, Kyria Xenobia."

"More in the Old Bushmill's, I think you mean." Zen smiled wider when the old man's lips pursed at her reference to the Irish whisky Damon had been drinking.

"He is Apollo's son, Kyria. He is much used to being boss and clearing all obstacles."

"And being full of himself, as Apollo was," Zen pointed out, moving toward the driver's side.

Yanos's lips twitched. "That too, Kyria."

Zen leaned over and kissed the grizzled cheek. "Take care of my boys, Yanos."

"That I will do, Kyria. I will not let them out of my sight." He held the car door for her and closed it behind her after she slid behind the wheel.

"So far you've kissed every male in the place but your husband," Damon complained, hitting the dashboard.

"Not true." Zen slipped the car into gear and headed down the driveway. "I kissed most of the men at the wedding, not all." She bit her lip when he growled. "And, as I recall, I kissed you five minutes ago. How could you forget that."

"I recall every kiss and embrace we've ever shared, every moment of our lovemaking. Shall I tell you about the first time? We sailed all day on my schooner, then anchored out from the dock—way out, as I remember."

Zen's palms grew damp. "There's no need to go into it now."

"Oh, but there is, my wife. You were mine then. You wanted me to take you. You asked me to make love to you, said that you wanted me to be your first and only love. Do you remember?"

Damon's words, like velvet-covered steel, seemed to pierce her very core and arouse all her desires once again. He talked on and on, recalling their lovemaking in excruciating detail, making her burn all over for him.

Even as she sought to concentrate every effort on driving, Zen recalled her younger self, as she had been then. She envisioned a twenty-year-old Zen as she followed Damon into the cabin, where they were going to change into dry clothes after having gone swimming. Then they would eat dinner.

Damon had gone to the bow of the boat, leaving the cabin for her.

Zen had removed her bikini top, but instead of taking off the bottom and showering, she had leaned against one of the bunks and looked out the window over the water. She felt like one of the luckiest people in the world because Damon Aristides was paying attention to her, because he looked at her as though he wanted to possess her. She didn't hear him enter the cabin, but when she heard him gasp, she knew he was behind her.

"I'm sorry, little one, I thought you'd changed. I'll be on deck—"

"Don't go, Damon." Zen whirled around to face him, and his eyes riveted at once on her breasts. Instead of hiding herself, she took a deep breath and pushed her shoulders back, wanting him to keep looking at her. She had been repelled by the thought of other men touching her . . . but she ached for Damon's caress.

"Zen . . ." Damon cleared his throat, his voice taut with tension.

"I want you, Damon. Is that so very bad?" she had said in a low voice.

"No, my angel. But you're so young. We'll wait a couple of years."

"Years?" Zen had wailed, catapulting herself across the cabin and against his bare chest. "I don't want to wait. You'll grow tired of me and want someone else."

"Not a chance," Damon had whispered, his body curving protectively over hers, his hands coming up to clutch her bare waist.

His mouth brushed her hair, and she lifted her face for his kiss.

Instead, he had lifted her off the floor and said against her mouth, "Love, are you sure? I can't... I won't—"

"I want you to love me, Damon."

"Dear God, you're a child... but I must have you," he murmured, his hands pressing her lips tightly against him, still holding her high off the floor.

"I love being so tall." Zen giggled, biting his chin, licking his cheek.

"Do you, darling?" Damon's voice was rough. "And I love it when you taste me."

"Oh, Damon, I want to keep you," she had whispered, moving restlessly in his arms.

"Yes, my little one..." He stripped the bikini bottom from her and carried her to the larger forward cabin, where he placed her on the king-sized bed. He stood back, and his eyes roved hotly over her naked body. "Your skin... and hair... your lovely breasts. I'll be gentle, my little one."

And he had been, loving her with his mouth and hands until she was on fire for him. She hardly felt the moment of discomfort when he penetrated her fully.

"Damon!" she had called out to him, her back arching as wave upon wave of love filled her and overflowed.

"Yes, my little one, I'm here." He had chuckled as he held her close. "My little voluptuary, I'm here with you."

She stayed with him through the night. It had frightened yet exalted her to know that Damon couldn't seem to get enough of her.

That summer they were together every minute...

Zen shook herself from her reverie, blinking at the Manhattan traffic.

"Even at twenty-five you were tricky. When I thought you were mine, you left me. Turn here and go up Park," Damon instructed.

"Me? Tricky? As I recall, you intimated that I would be the only woman in your life. Well, what do you call Cherry Crawford... not to mention other women associated with you in the tabloids?"

"You walked out on me, Xenobia Driscoll Aristides. You'll never do that again."

Zen's temper flared. "Are you threatening me?"

"If that's what it takes to keep you by my side, yes, I'm threatening you."

"You damn well can't threaten me," Zen said, fuming. She turned into the underground garage, anger making her just careless enough to come a hair too close to a cement column and scraping the side of the Ferrari.

"Xenobia..." Damon straightened in his seat and turned to glare at her. "What the hell are you doing to my car?"

"You are a most nerve-wracking man. I was doing fine until you began needling me." Zen bit her lip in remorse as she parked the car.

Damon flung open his door and stood there staring at the scratch. "Do you have any idea what it will cost to repair this?"

"Damon, I'm sorry. I'll pay for it." Zen struggled to unfasten her seat belt and climbed out of the car. "It was an accident."

"It's always an accident with you. I suppose I should be glad that you didn't ram us into a truck." Damon reeled ever so slightly as he reached for her.

Caught between laughter and chagrin, Zen pushed him away and whirled toward the elevator. The doors opened, she stepped in, and the doors closed before Damon reached her.

"Hey, wait—"

Damon's words were cut off as she was whisked upward at heart-stopping speed.

The elevator opened on a small foyer with two doors. One of the doors opened and a man with a mustache glanced out. She went to the other door and pushed her key into the lock. It wouldn't turn. The man stared at her.

"Are you a friend of the Winthrops?" he asked coldly.

"Who?"

"The Winthrops live in that apartment. Who are you?"

"Well, then is that—"

Before Zen could say any more, the elevator doors opened and a grim-faced Damon stepped out.

"There you are," he said, then turned to the man in the doorway. "Hello, Aubrey. She made a mistake and got on the wrong elevator."

"It's okay. As usual, Aristides, your taste in women is quite good." The man shut his door.

Zen glared after him. "Twit," she called. "I'm not one of his live-ins. I'm his wife."

"Will you keep your voice down and get in this elevator before Aubrey reports us both for breaking and entering," Damon said.

"Let him try!" Zen lifted her chin and raised her fist to knock on Aubrey's door, but Damon reached out and pulled her into the elevator.

Not releasing her, he punched the button for the garage. "Don't you ever listen? I called out that it was the wrong one."

"You sound more sober now," Zen commented, then frowned. "How the blazes was I to know that each tenant has his own elevator? That's disgusting."

"It's a good safety feature. When you didn't put your key into the elevator and didn't press the red light, as an invited guest would have done, Aubrey knew you were unauthorized. That's why he met you at the door. He has an alarm button that he could have pressed instead of opening the door. But he has a predilection for beautiful women."

"Do you think so?"

Damon's brow furrowed. "Do I think what?"

"Do you think I'm beautiful?"

"Yes." He led her out of the elevator and across the garage to another one. Inside, he punched the console. "That's been my problem for years. I think you're too damn beautiful."

Chapter 9

ZEN STARED AT him as they stepped into a foyer that led directly into his apartment. Surprised at this, she forgot what she had been about to ask him. She walked farther into the circular foyer, admiring the royal blue Chinese carpet with a sundial pattern in soft beige. The sunburst at the center was located directly under a crystal chandelier. "This is a bit opulent, isn't it?" she asked.

Damon strode past her down two steps to an oblong room, the floor of which was also scattered with Chinese carpets, these in mandarin red with geometric details in jade green. Damon poured himself half a glass of whisky. "Don't tell me. You want me to sell the carpets and give the money to indigent actors from the Abbey Players."

"There are no indigent actors at the Abbey Players," Zen retorted. "They're so good they always have work."

"Bull. There are always out-of-work actors and writers." Damon took a long swallow.

"I don't think that will do your headache any good."

He glared at her. "I don't have a headache."

"Early hangover?" she quizzed, earning another glower.

"I'm going to take a shower." He strode across the room, then stopped. "You may use the shower in the master suite. I'll use the other one."

"I never imagined eating my wedding supper with a tipsy bridegroom," Zen called out. His back stiffened but he didn't pause. Zen went into the master suite.

"Why did I provoke him?" she asked herself as she took off her clothes and stepped into the shower stall. "I was baiting him."

She soaped her body then took the time to brush her hair so that it rippled past her shoulders in red-gold curls.

She removed the silk kaftan that had been purchased from Charine and shook it out of the tissue paper.

From the box of jewelry that had been Eleni's and their mother's and that Damon had insisted was now hers, she selected antique earrings of topaz that swung like golden prisms against her cheeks. She stared at herself in the mirror. "Lord, you look as if you belong in a harem." From her dresser she took the vial of French perfume that Thag had ordered made especially for her. It was called Xenobia. She dabbed some on her neck and her wrists, ankles, and behind her knees.

Prepared for seduction, she crossed the short hall that led to the landing over the foyer and descended the curving stairs. Her Turkish slippers made only a whisper of sound as she entered the living room.

Damon was standing in front of the fireplace, a steaming mug in one hand, the other resting on the mantel. A burgundy silk robe was tied around his waist.

With great deliberation Zen stepped sideways until the light of a side lamp outlined her in the dimly lit room. Damon's shape was clearly etched by the flames in the fireplace, which cast odd shadows on his face, making him look like a demon from another world.

As Zen stepped forward, the swish of her kaftan brought his head up. In slow motion he turned, straightened, and looked her over from head to toe. "That's a very sexy outfit," he said at last, tipping the rest of whatever was in the mug down his throat.

"Charine suggested it." Zen coughed to clear her throat of its hoarseness.

"Did she? I must thank her." He moved a fraction of an inch closer. "You have such a tiny body, but so strong, so well made."

Zen's face warmed with embarrassment. "Damon, stop it. I feel as though your eyes might set my kaftan on fire." Her Turkish slippers seemed to be nailed to the floor.

Damon's laugh was harsh as he approached her, like a hunter who had trapped his quarry. "You're mine."

"And by the same token, you're mine," Zen replied boldly.

"Of course." They were face to face. Damon stood looking down at her without touching her. He bent to kiss her, his lips moving over her mouth with gentle insistence. "I have a surprise for you," he murmured.

"Another one? You've been surprising me all day." Zen smiled, then caught her breath as a deep flush darkened his face. "I didn't mean your drinking," she tried to explain.

Damon waved his hand to silence her, then took her hand and pulled her toward the table. "Maria sent us some wedding cake. She will freeze the top layer for our first anniversary, but she arranged to have the second tier brought to us. This is Greek honey cake." Damon opened a bottle of champagne and poured Zen a glass, then poured coffee into his mug.

"I like coffee," Zen said lamely.

"Not Turkish coffee you don't." Damon gave a hard laugh at her grimace. "And I've had more than enough alcohol."

"Damon, I didn't mean what I said—"

"What you said was the truth . . . and no woman deserves a drunk husband on her wedding night."

Zen accepted the piece of cake he cut for her and lifted

it to his mouth. Damon backed warily away. Zen laughed and shook her head. "I'll be very careful," she promised.

"Just put down the knife before you feed me." Damon grabbed both her wrists to steady her, then opened his mouth and took the piece she offered. "Ummm, good." He swallowed, and his tongue came out to catch a crumb at the corner of his mouth.

Watching him, Zen felt as if her heart had fallen a hundred feet and bounced up again. She couldn't imagine any other man in the world having such beautiful lips, such a lovely nose, such mesmerizing eyes. She loved his chin, and the laugh lines at the corners of his eyes. Had anyone else ever had such cheekbones? Without thinking, she raised her hand to trace his face.

"That gown should be registered with the police as a dangerous weapon," Damon muttered, letting his fingers rest on the light-as-air fabric. "You haven't changed at all since you were twenty."

"Yes, I have." Zen's breath came rapidly, as if she'd just run up a mountain.

"Oh, no, you haven't. I remember. Will you be afraid to spoil it by having children?" Damon bent over her and batted the dangling topaz earrings with his nose.

"I don't consider the changes in a woman's body that are brought about by childbearing to be bad." Zen's eyes fluttered shut as his mouth traveled to her neck.

"Do I take it then that we will have lots of children?"

"But you haven't said that you want them—I mean more of them."

"Having my own child grow in you, Xenobia? Oh, yes, I want that. But only if you're able to give birth safely. That you must discuss with your doctor."

"You want me to ask my doctor if I'm healthy enough to have children?" Zen gave a breathless laugh. "That's silly."

"I'm serious, Zen. We won't start a family unless I know that you're capable of carrying one without possibly harming yourself." Damon's expression was utterly serious. "We already have two boys. If we can't have others, then they will be enough."

"Damon, I..." Zen looked up at him, confused by the strained look on his face.

All at once he crushed her to him. "I don't want to talk about it anymore tonight."

He led her to the large U-shaped couch and sat down with her. "Watch." He pressed buttons on a console and a king-sized bed unfolded from the middle section.

Zen raised a skeptical eyebrow. "I've heard of passion pits. I suppose—"

"You suppose nothing. I had this installed after we announced our engagement. Listen." He pressed another button and music filled the room. "There's also a hidden television, a small bar—"

"All designed for seduction," Zen breathed. She laughed as his face turned dark crimson. "Damon, I don't believe it. There you go getting embarrassed again. You've been doing that all day, as though you were nervous." She stared up at him in sudden understanding. "I don't remember you ever being the least bit off balance about anything, but since the wedding..."

"My life has changed. I'm a husband and a father." He grinned down at her. "And remember, I have to be on my toes every minute. My bride is trying to do me in." He laughed when she poked him in the arm. "Of course, she calls her attempts to murder me accidents."

"They *are* accidents!" she exclaimed, feeling absurdly happy to be laughing with him, held close to his heart. "How do we get onto this humungous bed?"

"Easy." Damon swung her up into his arms, stepped down one step, and walked onto the bed. He sat down in the center, still holding Zen in his arms. "See?" His grin faded as he stared down at her. "You don't have anything on under that, do you, love?"

She shook her head.

"How farsighted of you." Damon relaxed his hold on her so that, although she remained in the V formed by his legs, he could now gaze at her reclining body.

"I don't like to walk on this lovely thing with my

shoes on," Zen said softly, held spellbound by his onyx eyes.

"Don't worry." Damon reached down and removed a slipper. Then he lifted her foot and nibbled on her toes.

"You have a foot fetish," Zen accused him.

"A fetish for your foot, yes." Damon sucked gently on her anklebone. "You have the trimmest body . . . Tastes good, too."

"Are you crazy?" Zen failed at repartee, her thoughts focused on the delicious sensations he was producing.

"Are you planning an accident that will cause brain damage and make me crazy?" Damon asked casually, removing the other slipper and kissing her little toe.

"That's very unkind." Zen clung to his shoulders as he pushed the kaftan up past her waist to her arms. She let go briefly as he lifted the garment over her head.

"Will you be warm enough, Zen?" Damon lowered her to the bedspread and leaned over her as he took off his robe.

"Warm." She nodded, looking up at him, loving the play of firelight on his face.

"I'll be your blanket," Damon growled into her neck.

"How kind of you." Zen felt as though she'd been disembodied and was floating around the room. She didn't seem to be connected to her body, though each separate part was clamoring for Damon's special attention. "Making love is so nice," she said, sighing.

"*Nice?* God, wife, you do have a talent for understatement."

"Thank you." Zen let her fingers furrow through his hair, loving the crisp feel of it. "Damon, will we leave it as a couch when the boys are with us?"

"What? What boys?" Damon seemed to have trouble focusing. "Xenobia, we're making love. We'll talk about the boys later."

"Lovely." Zen pulled the curling hairs on his chest. "I thought men couldn't make love when they had too much to drink." She nibbled on his chin.

"What?" Damon's hair stood on end where she had mussed it.

She couldn't suppress a giggle. Damon stared at her as if she had just popped in from Mars. "Don't you feel like making love?" he demanded sternly.

"Yes, I do." But she burst out laughing. He looked so silly glowering so darkly with his hair sticking up. Suddenly all her happiness bubbled up from inside her and broke forth in peals of laughter.

She sensed his angry withdrawal. "Don't go," she pleaded. "I really do want to make love." She shrugged one bare shoulder. "It's just that we've never been married before. I don't know why, but it's different now." A dark gleam flickered deep in his eyes. "I can't explain it, Damon. Don't be angry."

He pushed her down and leaned over her, his breath coming in harsh pants. "Why should I be angry about making love to Chuckles the Clown?" His body pressed against hers, his flesh touching her everywhere. "It's a new experience for me, too. I can't remember ever making love to a woman when she was laughing. No, don't talk. I don't want to hear any more."

She fell obediently silent as his hands and mouth explored her intimately, from her chin to her toes.

Their lovemaking was as forceful as always, but Zen sensed a restraint in Damon. When she began to speak, he would shush her, and soon the volcano that was between them erupted and spilled them out of themselves into a new dimension.

She fell asleep. When she woke sometime later, he was gone. She sat up in bed and punched the pillow. She wanted to get up and see if he was still in the apartment, but she was too tired. She fell into a restless sleep.

She woke again with a jerk, sitting bolt upright in bed, the sheet wrapped around her body like a shroud. She was still alone in the bed.

She rose with a sigh and went to the bathroom, where she ran the water until it was ice cold. She drank several glasses.

Where was Damon? Had he gone out?

She went into the bedroom and rummaged through her things until she found a light robe. She couldn't bear to look at the kaftan crumpled on the living room floor, where Damon had dropped it.

She wandered through the semidark apartment. A faint, predawn light filtered through floor-to-ceiling sheer curtains over a wall of windows in the living room. She was about to retrace her steps to the bedroom when she heard a muffled mutter that made her freeze in her tracks. Goose bumps covered her arms. Then she saw Damon sprawled face down on a couch on the other side of the living room, far from the king-sized bed.

She edged closer and took the glass from his hand, then lifted an empty bottle from the floor. "I hope you didn't drink all this, husband of mine, or you will have one aching head when you wake up." Zen bent to give him a closer look. Though he was breathing heavily, he seemed in fair shape, so she left him where he was.

She returned to the bed, but she didn't sleep. For hours she considered—and rejected—all sorts of possible explanations for Damon's uncharacteristic behavior. None of them made any sense. Was he so unhappy being married to her that he had to drink himself into a stupor? Had he felt that laughter during their lovemaking had emasculated him in some way? The Damon she knew was made of heartier stuff than that. She just didn't understand him.

At midmorning she gave up her attempt to sleep, and went to the kitchen to make a pot of coffee.

At first she was puzzled when she couldn't find a small percolator. Then she remembered that Damon had used one the night before. Rather than seek it out, and perhaps disturb him, she used a drip coffeemaker to prepare a full twenty-cup pot.

The phone rang as she was scrambling eggs for herself. She lifted it on the first ring.

Sophie answered. "Xenobia? Is that you, dear? I hated to wake you, but Thag and I thought we would take the boys up to Saratoga overnight and perhaps drive to Cooperstown to show them the Baseball Hall of Fame."

"Wouldn't it be better to take two nights, Sophie?"

Zen suggested, then smiled to herself when she heard her mother-in-law's sigh of relief.

"Yes, dear, it would. That's a wonderful idea. We'll take Seamus with us. David is so fond of him, and now so is Daniel. We just can't let him return to Ireland without doing a little sight-seeing now, can we?"

"Of course not. Kiss the boys for me, and we'll see you on Friday."

"Thank you, dear. And how is that son of mine?"

"Still sleeping," Zen said.

"My, my." Sophie was still chuckling when she hung up the phone.

Zen finished scrambling her eggs, then made herself some toast from homemade raisin bread the housekeeper had left.

"Is the coffee for anyone?"

Startled, Zen dropped the toast and whirled around. Damon was standing in the doorway, a towel wrapped around his waist, his feet, legs, and chest bare, his hair glistening wet.

"It's for you, Dracula," Zen said with forced lightness. "But I think you would do better with a transfusion."

"Thank you, bride of Frankenstein." Damon winced when she laughed. "Why is it I never noticed that you have a macabre sense of humor? Maybe because I spent so much time dodging the barbed words you were firing at me, and trying to survive your attempts to kill me."

Zen placed a mug of coffee in front of him. "If you're referring to the few times you had unfortunate accidents—"

"Accidents! How I hate that word! Damn, Zen, did you have to bang that pot on the table?"

"I did not bang it. It's glass. I would never bang glass."

Damon closed his eyes in resignation and sipped his coffee.

"Head hurt?" Zen inquired, munching on toast.

"Yes. Could you kindly stop chewing so loudly?"

"Touchy, touchy." Zen placed some of her scrambled

eggs in front of him. He glared at them, then at her.

"Remove that garbage."

"Damon, I'm sorry that you have a hangover, but it's your own fault and—"

"Don't lecture. May I please have some more coffee?"

Zen poured some, and Damon drank it in silence, then pushed his chair back from the table.

"What shall we do today?" Zen quizzed his retreating back.

He stopped but didn't turn to face her. "I thought we were going back to the house."

"We don't have to. Your mother called and said that she and Thag are taking the boys to Saratoga, I suppose to see the battlefield there, and then perhaps to Cooperstown. Sophie felt that since Seamus—"

"Seamus?" Damon interrupted. "Is he still here?" He rubbed an index finger across his forehead.

"Yes. Your mother didn't want him to return to Ireland without seeing something of the country," Zen explained.

"Dandy."

"So what would you like to do. After all, this *is* our honeymoon."

"I'm not the one who needs to be reminded of that." Damon glared at her.

"If you're referring to my laughing last night—"

"I'd rather not discuss it."

"I just want you to know that I'm sorry you misunderstood—"

"I misunderstood nothing. Excuse me, I'd like to get dressed."

"Hardhead," Zen muttered, taking her cup and plate to the sink. She washed the skillet by hand in a sinkful of suds.

She wandered aimlessly around the apartment, checking each room, deciding that she didn't feel comfortable in such stark surroundings.

"Change it if you wish," Damon said behind her in the study. She dropped the Eskimo whalebone she'd been examining.

"Will you stop doing that? I could have broken this!"

"So? It's yours. Replace it." Damon shrugged and handed her the carving. "You don't like the apartment as a whole, do you?"

"No. It's a bit too modern for me."

"Then redecorate it. You have unlimited funds now, my love." The sardonic twist of his lips disturbed her. What new product of his imagination was plaguing him? "Would you like to take a walk?" he suggested. "We're close to Central Park."

"Are you sure you're feeling—"

"I'm fine."

Zen opened her mouth to protest his rudeness, but the bullish expression on his face silenced her. "Yes, I'd like to take a walk," she said.

They got their coats and rode down in the elevator. As they approached Central Park, Zen saw that the trees were coming into full leaf. The greenery gave the park a fresh, bright look.

They wandered in silence along winding paths near the pond, watching the joggers and strollers who passed. Soon they left the park and headed down Fifth Avenue.

There was a cold bite in the air. Zen was upset to see a stern expression on his face. She took hold of his arm, tucking herself close to his side.

He looked down at her. "If you're cold, we can go back."

"No, I like to walk. In Ireland everyone walks. My hand was cold; that's all."

Damon's mouth softened, and he held her hand warmly. "I haven't walked in Manhattan in a long time. I forgot how beautiful New York is in the springtime."

"It's a wonderful city. I missed it when I was in Ireland."

"Was that all you missed?" His probing gaze told her he meant the question seriously.

"No, that's not all I missed." Zen felt as light as sunshine when he smiled at her.

"The fresh air has cleared my head," he admitted

"Then it must have strong powers, indeed," Zen said, teasing. She looked up warily to find him chuckling.

"What a tongue you have. I must be masochistic to take you on for life."

"Is it for life?" she asked shyly. "Marriage is a very disposable item these days."

"Not ours." Damon tugged her close to his side so that their bodies bumped together gently.

All at once the spring air seemed ten degrees warmer. Zen felt welcoming heat penetrate to her very core.

Damon lifted his hand and hailed a taxi. They climbed inside.

"Where are we going?" Zen asked as he pulled her into his arms.

"Wait and see," he whispered into her ear. "We might as well enjoy the short time away from our sons. Don't you agree?"

"Yes." She smiled up at him, not caring where the cab was going as long as Damon was with her and he wasn't angry with her.

She glanced around her from the shelter of Damon's arms. "Oh, we're in Greenwich Village, aren't we. Isn't that Washington Square? Where . . . ?" She fell silent as the taxi pulled to the curb, and Damon helped her onto the sidewalk. She looked up at a sign over a store that said Village Deli.

"Do you remember when we came here?" Damon asked behind her.

"Yes." Zen leaned against him. "I had come into Manhattan on the bus from school. You met me and brought me here and fed me. Then you dropped me at your apartment because you had to go back to the office. That night—"

"We went to a show, then to a club to dance." Damon led her into the deli and ordered bagels and lox, coleslaw, and coffee. They sat on soda-fountain chairs at a miniscule table.

"I was very embarrassed because I had to wear a plain blouse and skirt to the show and the club." Zen closed her eyes as she forked coleslaw into her mouth.

"I thought you looked perfect." Damon offered her some salmon and laughed when she smacked her lips.

"I was very impressed by all the people who came up to speak to you and call by name," she said. "I had never seen so many celebrities before."

"I don't remember anyone except you." Damon rested his chin on his folded hands and stared at her. "You were a doll—too young for me but a doll."

"I wasn't too young for you," Zen said indignantly.

"I was twenty-eight and a man. I had finished school and already made my first million."

Zen stared into his dark eyes and forgot what she had intended to say in rebuttal.

"Why did you leave me?" His low words started her heart pounding. Suddenly the tone of the conversation had changed to one of utter seriousness.

"I...I..." Zen didn't have an answer. All at once she didn't know why she had left him—except that fear had chased her across the Atlantic.

"After you went to Ireland, my mother explained my aunt's part in sending you away. I directed all of my anger at you for running away from me, and my feelings toward her changed, too." Damon smiled at her. "How she hated the women in my life! I think that was part of the reason why she insisted on my writing to you." He shook his head. "I didn't want to ask you to come back. My pain had grown numb over the years, and I didn't want to open old wounds."

"I thought I hated you," Zen admitted painfully. "But when I came back and saw you, I knew I'd been lying to myself all that time."

"Let's get out of here."

They paid the bill and left quickly, hailing a cab to take them uptown.

"Have we been fools, Damon?" Zen whispered.

"Fifteen kinds of a fool, my love." He kissed her lingeringly, his mouth insistent, demanding.

"Damon . . ." Zen loved the feeling of being enveloped

in his arms. "When we were separated, I had nightmares that you would never hold me again, never love me. In my dreams I chased after you, called to you..." She looked up at him, and realized with surprise that there were tears on her cheeks.

"Zen, my darling, we'll never be separated again," Damon vowed, his arms tightening around her.

Chapter 10

THAT NIGHT THEY went to see a show, a rollicking, racy musical that made Zen laugh and tap her feet. After the show she and Damon were slow to leave their seats.

"Relax," Damon said. "It's raining. Everyone will be fighting for cabs. Once the crowd thins the car will be waiting to take us to Dominie's." Damon's eyes ran over Zen. "Not that I care to take you anywhere, dressed as you are. You look like a pink moonbeam." His dark eyes seemed to touch every part of her. "I would never have picked that color to go with your hair, but it looks great." He toyed with the cluster of curls that she'd swept behind her ear and fastened with a comb encrusted with pink crystal.

"I don't often wear rose, but Charine and your mother thought it would be a good color for me." Feeling shy under his intense gaze, Zen tried to smooth down the muted pink ruffles that decorated the knee-length hem of her strapless dress. The simple bodice was cut straight across the top of the bust. She wore medium-heeled silver sling-back shoes and carried a matching purse. She carried a crocheted lace shawl that one of Damon's great aunts had given her.

"You are the most beautiful woman in this theater, and if you weren't my wife already, I would seduce you and make you mine."

Zen's skin blushed as pink as her dress, and her eyes darted left and right to see if anyone had heard what Damon said. "You Greeks say the most outrageous things," she admonished her husband.

"I'm an American, as you are, my lovely wife." Damon caught her bottom lip with his teeth and nipped it gently.

"Stop. People are looking."

"Let them." Damon grinned at her, unrepentent.

A few moments later he rose and pulled her up with him, his hand tucked under her elbow. With great care he draped the shawl around her shoulders. "Will you be warm enough?"

Blue fire was coursing through her veins at his simple touch. Zen nodded. "I think I'll be comfortable."

Damon kissed her bare shoulder where the shawl had slipped. "Tell me if you're not. I'm more than willing to warm you."

"How kind of you," she said lightly, though her heart was pounding out of control.

They made their way past stragglers in the lobby to a cluster of people who were huddled under the marquee to keep dry.

Damon held her in the curve of his arm and peered up and down the street for the limousine. which cruised to a stop at the curb. The driver held the car door open directly under the canopy. They hurried into the warm, dry interior and settled gratefully against the leather seats.

Ensconced in Damon's arms, Zen was content to watch the rain streak down the window. They could drive to hell and back. She didn't care a long as she was with her husband.

Dominie's proved to be a popular club. People standing, sitting, and leaning everywhere. The dance floor, though larger than average, was packed.

"Good evening, Mr. Aristides. How nice to see you and—" The maître d's plastic smile barely faltered as he tried to remember Zen's name.

"Good evening, Leonard. This is my wife, Mrs. Aristides. Darling, meet Leonard." Damon's introduction was cool, almost aloof.

The maître d' led them to a booth screened by a row of plants. "Your table, Mr. Aristides," Leonard said stiffly.

Zen let her shawl fall from her shoulders to her elbows. "He sensed that you're angry with him. Is it because you wanted him to be more discreet, and not act taken aback because you weren't with one of your... er...friends?" She rested her chin in her hands and watched as he stared out at the dancing couples.

"Yes." He turned toward her. "And damn you for realizing that, Xenobia. I don't relish having a wife who reads my mind."

"And I don't like the fact that you've come here before with other women," Zen retorted.

A waiter arrived with mineral water for her and whisky for Damon.

"But I couldn't forget you, Xenobia." Damon stared into his drink, then reached over and took a sip of hers. "Ummm, that's good. After last night, that's probably what I should be drinking." He looked askance at her. "Do you think I'm trying to change the subject?"

Zen laughed. "Yes, but at least we're talking. About how we feel, how we react to each other." She shrugged. "I consider that a move in the right direction."

Damon entwined her fingers with his. "I won't tell you about all the women I had when we were apart. I will tell you, though, that I tried everything, every trick I could think of, to blot you from my mind. I hated not being able to. It made me feel weak. I woke up in the middle of the night with your face filling my mind, your name on my lips."

"And another woman in your bed." Zen finished for him. But her words held no censure. She understood a little better now the demons he had been fighting.

"Yes," Damon admitted. "And another woman in my bed." He lifted his glass and tipped some whisky down his throat. "I wanted those women to mean something to me. I wanted to find a woman, any woman, I could take home to mother and marry. I thought I didn't give a damn who she was...but I couldn't bring myself to do it."

They sat in thoughtful silence. When the waiter returned, Damon ordered a light supper of broiled prawns on a bed of endive. They drank a sharp, crisp Riesling.

After they had eaten, Damon squeezed Zen's hand. "Shall we dance?" he suggested. "Please."

As she followed Damon to the floor, Zen remembered a younger Zen Driscoll going to a club with Damon and dancing all night. How surprised and pleased she had been to discover that he knew all the latest steps.

Now Damon held her close, and they moved together to the slow, sensuous rhythm. When the tempo changed to a tango, Zen shook her head and laughed, "I've never danced the tango," she protested. But Damon led her effortlessly and twirled her dramatically. Zen laughed breathlessly as he swung her away from him then pulled her back.

"Haven't you ever tangoed, my love?" Damon asked, grinning at her. "You do it very well." He guided her with firm but light pressure.

She could feel every muscle in his thighs as he held her. "My goodness," she exclaimed.

"A very sensual dance, isn't it?" Damon laughed down at her, his eyes twinkling.

"Damon Aristides, you should be ashamed of yourself." Despite their recent openness with each other, Zen felt a stab of envy at the thought of the other women who had enjoyed her husband's skillful dancing.

He leaned close to her as the music slowed to a ballad. "I was never quite as aware of a woman's body as I am tonight, my angel," he muttered into her hair. "However much I wanted a woman, I was never in danger of losing control. With you I'm never in control." He paused to maneuver around another couple. "Did you want many men when we were apart?" At her skeptical look, he added, "I'm being masochistic tonight, as Greeks often are." He sighed. "I want to hear—but I don't want to hear."

Zen met his smoldering gaze. "There were several men. I liked their company. I might have married Seamus eventually. He likes David very much, and he would have been kind to me. But I saw marriage to Seamus as something that would happen in the future." Zen wrapped her arms around his neck. "We're married now. We have advantages other married people don't have. We've had our baptism of fire. We won't be quick to part."

"We will never part, Xenobia, no matter what happens." Damon seemed to be all around her, enveloping her in a sense of warmth and protection.

Just then, an all-too-familiar voice carried across the room. "Damon," Cherry Crawford caroled. "How sweet! You brought your bride to Dominie's. Did she want to meet all your former mistresses, darling?"

"Not all of them Cherry," Damon drawled, "just a few."

Zen leaned against his chest, loving the steady beat of his heart under her cheek. She regarded Cherry with indifference, content to let Damon lead where once she would have demanded independence. Where once she would have demanded to be heard, now she was content to wait in silence.

"Carter and I will join you," Cherry said, turning away. "I know where your table is."

Damon's body stiffened under Zen's hand. "Shhh, don't worry," she said. "We won't be staying long anyway." She smiled up at him, feeling lazy and confident.

A look of amazement furrowed Damon's brow. Then his tough-tender smile transformed his face, moving her almost to tears. "You don't give a damn if she joins us, do you?" he said softly.

"I don't care if she invites the whole world to our

door. We'll always be alone if we choose to be, won't we?"

"Yes, my love," Damon's eyes stayed fixed on hers.

"Damon, lean down. You're so tall, you know, and I want to whisper to you." Zen chuckled, then stroked him when she felt him stiffen at the sound. "I love you, Damon—desperately, totally, completely. I've loved you since the first moment we met at Eleni's and Davos's wedding rehearsal." She laughed again, pressing her nail into his chin. "I laughed last night because I was so happy." She paused and glanced around her. Damon had eyes only for her. "I'll tell you more later when we're alone, shall I?" she suggested with an impish grin.

"Please." Damon kissed her forehead.

"We should sit down. People are staring at us." Zen struggled to control an insane desire to laugh out loud.

"Will you believe me if I tell you that I've loved you since before you loved me?" Damon grinned at her open mouth and began to lead her from the floor.

"How can that be?"

"I have something to tell you later, too," he replied, laughing now, too.

"Keep careful watch on me or I might put something in Cherry's drink to get rid of her." Zen muttered just as they reached the table.

"Darling Damon, how nice to hear you laughing like that." Cherry bared her teeth in an insincere smile. "You know Carter Siddons, don't you?"

"Siddons," Damon nodded. "This is my wife, Xenobia Aristides. Darling, you know Cherry, and this is Carter Siddons."

"How do you do." Zen was about to slide into the booth, but Cherry stopped her.

"Do let Damon sit here, Zen. I refuse to call you that horribly ponderous name that Damon calls you. But I'm sure you understand that Damon and I have so much to say to each other."

But Damon's firm hand on Zen's arm, kept her at his side. He gestured to the waiter. "Please bring them whatever they choose and put it on my tab," he instructed.

He reached for Zen's shawl. "So sorry, but Zen and I are tired." Damon smiled at tight-lipped Cherry and affable-looking Carter. "Have a nice evening." The bored look on his face made Zen bite her lip to hold back a grin.

They left hand in hand. Their wide smiles earned a wary glance from the maître d'.

"Leonard thinks we're smashed," Zen said as she and Damon waited for their car to arrive.

"I feel more drunk than I ever have in my life."

On the way home Zen sang a song in Irish.

"What does it mean?" Damon asked, cuddling her.

"Oh, like most Irish songs, it's about life, death, and eternal love. The Irish are so romantic." Zen yawned.

"Are you tired?" Damon's voice held a note of disappointment.

"Not a bit. Just so relaxed that I feel as if my bones have collapsed." She looked up at him. "You've set me free, Damon. How many free people do you know?"

"Do you mean how many people do I know who are in love?" Damon asked her.

"Wise man." Zen rested her head on his chest, feeling so protected, so cared for, yet so strong and unencumbered. "It's really too bad that there are no more dragons to be slain. I could handle two of them tonight, with one hand tied behind my back."

"A lady knight." Damon sounded amused.

When the car pulled up in front of their apartment building, Zen followed Damon out of the vehicle and turned to face the driver. "Thank you for the lovely ride. It was wonderful."

The driver nodded seriously. "Thank *you*, ma'am." He doffed his cap and drove away as Damon and Zen strolled into the foyer.

"He thinks I'm tipsy." Zen clamped a hand over her mouth to smother her laughter.

"He doesn't understand that you've discovered the fountain of all happiness," Damon said, ushering her into the elevator.

"You." Zen twined her arms around his waist.

"Darling, do you know that you make me feel very humble?" The elevator doors opened to their apartment, and they wandered into the living room. "I feel as if I should pay the national debt or do something equally grand. I have so much to pay back. Do you understand what I mean?"

"I know exactly what you mean." Zen threw her arms wide. "Sometimes you feel guilty for having found so much love when you know how rare it is. Yet love is the common denominator of life, the most basic thing there is." She whirled to face Damon. "Are we getting philosophical?" she asked, her eyes wide.

"We are." He answered sagely. He led her to the couch and pressed the button to open it into the mammoth bed. His eyes fused on her body and surveyed her slowly, sending white heat pulsing through her. "You look glorious," he said huskily.

"I should hope so." Zen laughed, then clapped a hand over her mouth again. "I'm trying not to laugh, but love has a weird effect on me. All the tittering, smirking, giggling that I didn't do all those years we were apart is spilling out of me. You see"—she took a deep breath to steady herself—"love is strange. It makes you look glorious. It makes you chortle like a teenager. But"—she held up an index finger—"only if you're loved back." Her bottom lip began to tremble. "Last night I realized that Damon Aristides loves me." She shrugged one bare shoulder, bringing Damon's gaze to it. "I couldn't handle such a momentous realization." She blinked at Damon. "Did you ever laugh at something foolish and keep on laughing, not because your foolishness was funny but because your insides were celebrating? Mine were celebrating the stupendous revelation that you loved me." The words were pouring out of her. "Until that moment, I thought I could live without your loving me. Then I discovered that . . . that you pull the sun up in the morning for me, that the moon is full because you touch me." She took another shaky breath. "Now do you understand why . . . why I was laughing?"

Damon looked at her, unable to speak, a dark red

staining his cheeks. "Will you be my wife?" he asked finally.

Zen chuckled. "I am your wife, silly."

"I'm going to ask you that question every day for the rest of our lives, Xenobia Driscoll Aristides."

He swept her up in his arms and stepped into the middle of the bed, sat down, and held her on his lap. "Now, where were we? Ah, yes. I was just thinking about kissing your knee. Have I told you, my love, that you have sexy knees?"

Zen giggled and cuddled closer to him, closing her eyes in rapture as his tongue touched the back of her leg. "No, but you must tell me that every day, too. Oh, I'm going to love being married to you." Her eyes popped open when he fell still beside her.

He was regarding her intently. "On your birthday— I think it was when you turned twenty-six and you had been gone a year—I was here in my apartment alone, preparing to get drunk, as I did every year on your birthday."

"You did?" Zen grieved for the pain he had suffered. She cradled his head against her. "I won't let you be hurt anymore."

His tongue caressed her shoulders. "There's nothing in this world that can destroy me if you stay with me, my love."

"Me, too." Zen gazed at him with a solemn promise in her eyes. Then her mouth curved in a smile.

"Here comes Chuckles the Clown again," Damon murmured, easing her onto her back in the bed, his grin widening when she began to giggle. "You are my love challenge," he said.

"Do you think you can make me stop laughing?"

Damon's soft smile conveyed a hunger she was eager to satisfy. "I will enjoy the challenge, my darling albatross."

"What?" Zen struggled to a sitting position. "What are you saying? You're *my* albatross, not the other way around, Damon."

"So you told me at the cottage one night in your sleep.

Whether I stay or leave you, you said, I'm your albatross." In one gentle motion, he pulled her bodice down to bare her breasts. "Ummm, so lovely . . . so tasty." He leaned over to suck her nipple.

"Yeeek! Damon Aristides, stop it. We're talking," Zen moaned.

"So talk, darling. I won't stop you." Damon put his arms around her waist as he shifted to the other breast.

"Did I really talk in my sleep?" Zen ran her fingers through his hair.

"Many times. You were often restless, my sweet, so I held you. The night I read "The Rime of the Ancient Mariner" to the boys, you called me your albatross in your sleep."

"I thought about it when I woke up, too—how the bird flew around the ship and the winds filled the sails, then the bird was killed and the winds died and bad luck followed the Mariner." Damon's arms tightened on her. "Without you, nothing went well in my life. Oh, it carried on. David made me happy, my career was satisfying. But there was no luster, no freedom, no deep delight, no joy." Zen grew frustrated as she tried to express her feelings to Damon. "What's the matter with me? I talk constantly these days."

"Go on, my darling." Damon kissed her navel. "I love hearing that I'm important to you."

"Important? What a milksop word! Try intrinsic to my life, indigenous to my being," Zen expostulated, then giggled. "I'm doing it again, philosophizing." She looked up at him. "How many of the women you made love to also expounded on philosophy?"

"Not more than ten." Damon chuckled when she punched his arm.

"Damon," Zen said, "what were you going to tell me about getting drunk on my twenty-sixth birthday?"

Damon rolled over onto his back, placing his head in her lap. "My mother had been nagging me to get you to bring David back to see her. As usual, I told her that I felt it was up to you to make the first move.

Well, that night, as I opened my bottle of whisky and prepared to drown my sorrows, it suddenly hit me that I had no chance of ever having you again as long as you were in Ireland, that you might even marry over there, and then you would be completely lost to me. In that moment I decided I would fight, fair or foul, to get you—and that I would win." He looked up at her and fell silent.

She leaned over him, letting her red-gold hair drape around him. "And what did you mean when you said that you loved me first?"

"I like this," he whispered, "being curtained by your hair. I've never felt so secure. We're good for each other, aren't we, my love."

"Tell me," Zen urged, her fingers caressing his face.

"When Eleni and Davos began dating, you must have been about seventeen or eighteen. I was down at the dock with my boat when they asked to go sailing with me. Eleni was always a good sport about doing whatever Davos wanted. She sailed even though I don't think she liked it."

"She didn't," Zen recalled.

"On this particular day we jibed unexpectedly, and Eleni's purse slid across the deck. Her wallet fell out, open to a picture of a woman in a bikini, and I asked who it was. It was you. Eleni and Davos were so busy gathering her belongings before they blew away that they didn't notice when I pocketed the picture."

"You did?" Zen's nerve endings hummed with joy.

Damon reached for the jacket he had tossed aside. He fumbled through his wallet and drew out a worn snapshot of a younger Zen, smiling directly into the camera. He dumped his wallet upside down, and other pictures of her fell onto the bed, photos of her in her early twenties, then a newspaper picture of her just before she left for Ireland.

"This was all I had of the woman I loved," he said hoarsely. "I was ashamed of loving an eighteen-year-old girl, but I did love you. I saw you at nineteen when you swam in the state meet in college. I went alone to watch you. I wanted you even then."

"I wish I'd known that."

"Oh, God," Damon groaned, kissing the inner curve of her breast. "I didn't want you to know then. No one ever knew. And when I met you through Davos and Eleni, I pretended it was the first time I'd seen you."

They fell into a long, thoughtful silence as Zen assimilated this new knowledge of him.

"Damon, your mother approached me once during the court battle to take David to Ireland. But I thought it was to castigate me further. I was young and raw with loving you. I see now that she might have been trying to mend fences."

"I forgave her long ago, because I saw how upset she was about what my Aunt Dalia said to you. But I ignored all of her pleas to get in touch with you. I don't know why. I guess I was too stubborn and proud to admit that I'd been wrong to let you go away. Then, when you returned from Ireland, I was determined to move heaven and earth if need be to win you back." He chuckled. "I must say, working through David was simpler."

"Devious man."

He nodded, his thick hair tickling her bare breasts. "Angel, your pink dress is getting badly wrinkled. Let me take it off you. After all, I'll want to see you in this gown many more times. Of course, only when we're dining alone."

"Silly," Zen cooed, lifting her arms so that he could ease the dress over her head. She was wearing a half-slip of pink silk, pink silk panties, and a pink garter belt and stockings. Damon's eyes were riveted to her. Her hand touching his arm recalled him from his contemplation of her.

"Would you hire me as your lady's maid?" he asked.

"Job sharing," Zen said dreamily. "I'll be your valet, and you can be my maid. What's a fair salary?"

"No salary, just fringe benefits." Damon swallowed hard as he unhooked each garter and rolled the stockings down her legs.

"Is this what the well-dressed wife of Damon Aristides should wear? Dangling earrings and nothing else?" Zen giggled as Damon urged her down on the bed and stretched out next to her.

"Yes. Now, about me making you stop laughing . . ." Damon had a devilish leer on his face as his mouth moved closer and smothered the chortle just escaping her lips. His tongue filled her mouth, tangling playfully with hers. His hands skimmed over her, reacquainting themselves with each dip and curve of her body. He sought out each pleasure spot, and she gasped when he touched her, first with his hands, then with his mouth.

"Damon . . ." She heard her voice as if from far away. It seemed to belong to someone else entirely. She opened her eyes to find his black gaze drawing her into a sensual vortex.

Sensation upon sensation built within her in an exquisite crescendo. She was lost in him, one with him, enveloped and overwhelmed by him, body and soul. Again and again he caressed her flesh to throbbing readiness, then calmed his touch and soothed her restless yearning, only to build it to fever pitch once more.

At last, their bodies damp and straining, he moved to take complete possession of her. His thrusts were slow and powerful and made her cry out with every stroke. She clung to his shoulders like a drowning person to a lifeline in a turbulent sea.

As he moved faster and faster within her, she lost all sense of herself.

She was climbing steadily on a still sharper ascent. There, everything stood still, teetering on a splendid brink, pausing in breathless ecstasy. And then she tumbled, tumbled, and was flung high up on a dry beach, still clutching Damon in her arms.

Long moments later, side by side, nose to nose, Damon whispered, "Now I understand why you laughed. I hadn't realized how much joy was bottled up in me, my love." He shook his head. "I'd watched you with the boys and felt such a complete happiness, especially the day you were trying to head the ball in soccer."

"What do you mean, trying?" Zen's eyes flashed.

"You were good," he assured her. "And no wonder, since you were such a tomboy when you were young." Damon rubbed her back.

"And you know all about that because you were there for some of it."

"Yes, I was there. Whenever I could drive upstate, I attended your meets. And no one knew, not even you."

"Maybe I knew deep inside. I used to wish that I had parents who were watching me. Sometimes I would imagine that the cheering was for me. Did you cheer?"

"Oh, yes, my dove, I cheered." Damon pulled her onto his chest. "Shall we take a shower?"

"Together?"

"Of course. You're my wife, and I'm not letting you out of my sight."

"Good plan." She allowed him to pull her up.

He was momentarily distracted by her bouncing breasts. "I like it when they do that," he said.

Zen shook her head. "I do feel sorry for the women that David and Daniel put their eye on, because I think they are just like you."

"Do you?" Damon preened, flexing his muscles, drawing her eyes to his body. "Good. Then I hope they find someone just like you, someone to drive them mad." He swept her into his arms and headed toward the bathroom.

On the way, Zen spied a bronze sculpture on a Sheraton table. "Oh, how beautiful!" She scooped up the bronze as Damon walked past and began to examine its intricate detail. But her movements caused Damon to lose stride and stagger. He jostled Zen in his arms, and her tenuous grip on the sculpture loosened. The statue slipped from her fingers. "Oh!" Zen gasped.

"Aaaaagh! Xenobia, my toe!" yelled her naked husband, putting her down abruptly.

"Oh, darling, are you hurt?" she cried. "Oh, let me see. Oh, dear, your toe is so red." Zen tried to get a closer look as Damon hopped around on one foot, holding the other foot in his hand.

"Don't you dare...call it an accident," he warned her, wincing in pain.

Once Zen was sure Damon was all right, she had a hard time containing the laughter that was bursting inside her. She clapped a hand to her mouth.

Damon glared at her as she ran from the room to find some soothing ointment. "Damn you, Xenobia," he shouted. "That had better not be laughter I hear. My toe *hurts*."

Zen returned moments later, still as naked as her glowering husband. "I don't suppose you'll believe that I love you more than anything or anybody in the whole wide world," she said, kneeling in front of him to rub his toe.

"Oh, yes, I believe that. I just don't believe you will ever get over this propensity to do me harm." Damon pulled her to her feet. "Forget the toe. It isn't broken, and the shower will feel good on it." His eyes glinted with sensual mirth. "Our grandchildren will be horrified to hear how you tried to murder me on our honeymoon, strutting around unclothed and sexy."

"Then I'll tell them the terrible effect you have on me." Zen hesitated, caught by his hot gaze. Her mind went blank. "I forgot what I was going to say," she admitted.

They walked into the bathroom side by side, their arms around each other.

In the shower they began a game of love that continued in the bedroom.

"Do you want to eat?" Damon asked some time later as he lay sprawled next to Zen on the bed.

She regarded him lovingly. "I don't need food when I have you. You nourish me." The smile faded from her face as he continued to caress her. "You're my vitamins and minerals," she murmured.

"And you are all things to me, my albatross love," Damon muttered into her neck.

"No..." Zen's words were hoarse. "You're *my* albatross love."

All through the night their sensual discussion continued, neither one wanting to end it.

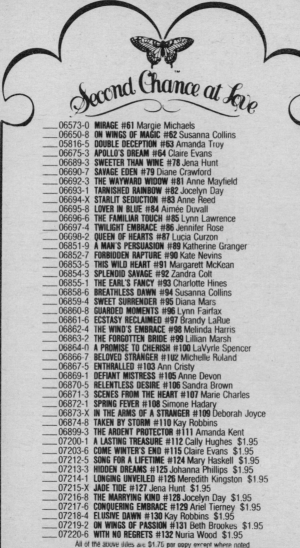

___ 07221-4	CHERISHED MOMENTS #133 Sarah Ashley	$1.95
___ 07222-2	PARISIAN NIGHTS #134 Susanna Collins	$1.95
___ 07233-0	GOLDEN ILLUSIONS #135 Sarah Crewe	$1.95
___ 07224-9	ENTWINED DESTINIES #136 Rachel Wayne	$1.95
___ 07225-7	TEMPTATION'S KISS #137 Sandra Brown	$1.95
___ 07226-5	SOUTHERN PLEASURES #138 Daisy Logan	$1.95
___ 07227-3	FORBIDDEN MELODY #139 Nicola Andrews	$1.95
___ 07228-1	INNOCENT SEDUCTION #140 Cally Hughes	$1.95
___ 07229-X	SEASON OF DESIRE #141 Jan Mathews	$1.95
___ 07230-3	HEARTS DIVIDED #142 Francine Rivers	$1.95
___ 07231-1	A SPLENDID OBSESSION #143 Francesca Sinclaire	$1.95
___ 07232-X	REACH FOR TOMORROW #144 Mary Haskell	$1.95
___ 07233-8	CLAIMED BY RAPTURE #145 Marie Charles	$1.95
___ 07234-6	A TASTE FOR LOVING #146 Frances Davies	$1.95
___ 07235-4	PROUD POSSESSION #147 Jena Hunt	$1.95
___ 07236-2	SILKEN TREMORS #148 Sybil LeGrand	$1.95
___ 07237-0	A DARING PROPOSITION #149 Jeanne Grant	$1.95
___ 07238-9	ISLAND FIRES #150 Jocelyn Day	$1.95
___ 07239-7	MOONLIGHT ON THE BAY #151 Maggie Peck	$1.95
___ 07240-0	ONCE MORE WITH FEELING #152 Melinda Harris	$1.95
___ 07241-9	INTIMATE SCOUNDRELS #153 Cathy Thacker	$1.95
___ 07242-7	STRANGER IN PARADISE #154 Laurel Blake	$1.95
___ 07243-5	KISSED BY MAGIC #155 Kay Robbins	$1.95
___ 07244-3	LOVESTRUCK #156 Margot Leslie	$1.95
___ 07245-1	DEEP IN THE HEART #157 Lynn Lawrence	$1.95
___ 07246-X	SEASON OF MARRIAGE #158 Diane Crawford	$1.95
___ 07247-8	THE LOVING TOUCH #159 Aimée Duvall	$1.95
___ 07575-2	TENDER TRAP #160 Charlotte Hines	$1.95
___ 07576-0	EARTHLY SPLENDOR #161 Sharon Francis	$1.95
___ 07577-9	MIDSUMMER MAGIC #162 Kate Nevins	$1.95
___ 07578-7	SWEET BLISS #163 Daisy Logan	$1.95
___ 07579-5	TEMPEST IN EDEN #164 Sandra Brown	$1.95
___ 07580-9	STARRY EYED #165 Maureen Norris	$1.95
___ 07581-7	NO GENTLE POSSESSION #166 Ann Cristy	$1.95
___ 07582-5	KISSES FROM HEAVEN #167 Jeanne Grant	$1.95
___ 07583-3	BEGUILED #168 Linda Barlow	$1.95
___ 07584-1	SILVER ENCHANTMENT #169 Jane Ireland	$1.95
___ 07585-X	REFUGE IN HIS ARMS #170 Jasmine Craig	$1.95
___ 07586-8	SHINING PROMISE #171 Marianne Cole	$1.95